Vengeance Is a Stranger

He was running from a man he had never seen, wildly driven by an uncontrollable fear of death. And even the Pacific Ocean was no barrier to his would-be murderer.

Sam Turk doubted that anyone remembered him after twenty years in prison for accidental murder. He was sure no one cared about his release—but someone did. Someone had tried to shoot him in the darkened streets of Amarillo. A stranger had asked about him in Santa Fe, then disappeared. In San Francisco the strange events continued. No matter where he ran he couldn't elude his relentless pursuer.

In desperation, Turk turned to an old-time Texan friend who was now the overseer of a huge cattle ranch in Hawaii. When he boarded the ocean steamer, Turk thought he had successfully eluded his unseen assailant. He soon found otherwise: whoever wanted him dead was still on his trail.

Set in exotic Hawaii at the turn of the century, here is an unusual novel of mystery and suspense, of cattle, cowboys, and courage.

 Look for the Double D Brand

JACK LEWIS

Vengeance
Is a
Stranger

DOUBLEDAY & COMPANY, INC. GARDEN CITY, NEW YORK

1966

All characters in this novel are fictitious with the exception of Ben Low, who introduced the paniolo to the American public in his rodeo appearance shortly after the turn of the century.

to
Ilse Lahn,
Agent, confidante . . . but, most important,
friend!

Vengeance Is a Stranger

One

Guns are like bad women. You might be able to leave them alone, but that doesn't make you forget them. A small, gray-haired man with a soft-voiced, friendly manner that hid his steel had told me that a long time ago. It had been four months ago in Huntsville, Texas. Four months there could be a lifetime.

As I stood in the cabin of the ship, looking down at the stag-handled Peacemaker and the worn, scuffed belt and holster that were bound snugly about the blue metal of the weapon, the warning behind the man's philosophical words jabbed at my brain. The words were still with me as I pushed the deadly bundle beneath some clothing and snapped shut the suitcase before pushing through the cabin door and out onto the sun-soaked deck. Then I forgot them.

The captain of the freighter, a black Irishman named O'Toole, stood at the rail shouting orders at the Hawaiian stevedores on the raw timber pier. Several of them struggled to get the heavy gangplank into place. Amidships, others worked bare to the waist, clad only in cheap cotton trousers. With the silent busyness of ants before a cloudburst, they hurriedly emptied the boxes and crates from the cargo nets which were dropped over the side. The heavier work was being done by the smaller men, all of whom had the narrow-eyed appearance of Orientals. Japanese, I judged, from my earlier talks with the captain.

The other ship was tied up at another new pier down the harbor. I had never seen it before, but I knew the name that stood out in stark-white lettering against its rusty, black hull. The sight of it caused the skin to tighten at the back of my neck, and there was a dull, empty feeling—the emptiness that is the bastard child of defeat—in the pit of my stomach.

"We'll be able to let you off in just a minute, Mister Turk," O'Toole declared, half turning and catching sight of me. His gaze went past me, seeing the ship at the other pier. He nodded toward it, his grin taking on a tinge of disgruntlement. He had seen me staring, knew I was wondering.

"The *Black Star*. Left San Francisco the day after we did. Tied up last night. Little faster vessel than us. Don't know how the owners of this tub expect me to compete with a ship that's almost three knots faster."

He shrugged his frustration and started to turn back to the rail, but my voice stopped him. My vocal chords were tight and the words seemed to catch on them, cling with the tenacity of a wood tick until I shook each of them off.

"They told me when I paid passage on your ship there wouldn't be another sailing for two weeks!"

"She was supposed to sail the day before us but got held up to take on some extra cargo. She gets all the big priority stuff, and we have to take the leavings." His tone was sympathetic as he went on: "We'll have you off here in a minute. Can't blame you for being jumpy. Rough trip."

He turned back to the railing, shouting orders at the dark-skinned men still struggling with the gangplank.

I realized my voice had been harsh. Accusing. But O'Toole wasn't running. There was the six gun hidden in my bag and the warning of the little gray man back in Huntsville. He hadn't been running either. All he had to do was come to work in the morning and sit behind a desk all day, telling other people how to handle their lives and what they had done that was wrong before. No. He had never had to run.

As I glanced about, the thought cut across my bitterness that Hawaii was not what I had expected. Robert Louis Stevenson's books had described it as a lazy, easy place where palm trees met the water, skies were constantly blue, people always happy.

On the wharf below me, a pair of stevedores were arguing, waving their arms at each other in wild threats, while O'Toole shouted at them in a tongue I didn't understand. Whatever the dialect, his tone was coated with curses. The men looked up at him abruptly, then went back to unloading a cargo net, ignoring each other with practiced surliness.

I had seen the Island first at dawn as we approached Hilo Harbor. The hard bulk of the volcano that the captain had called Mauna Kea came slowly out of the blue haze of night to meet us. As we drew into the harbor, I stood looking at the white expanse of sand that stretched up from the smooth water to clumps of coconut palms. The port town of Hilo had appeared as a small settlement gathered in a compact cluster of buildings that extended like welcoming arms to several piers that ringed the beach.

Now it looked different. The wharves were almost new, and there was an ugliness in the unaged lumber. Other raw, wooden buildings whose long, squat forms identified them as warehouses extended along the waterfront, while behind, the community resembled a boom town that had overextended itself and was trying desperately to fill in the vacancies between its scattered buildings. Some of the houses and business structures were of the same new, unpainted timber, while others, there longer, were fashioned with walls of woven palm fronds and boasted thatch roofs turned brown by wind, rain and the acid action of salt air. Hilo of 1906 was a small child who suddenly had discovered it could walk and was wobbling forward with the certainty born of overconfidence, not realizing that overbalance would send it sprawling in the dirt.

O'Toole dropped the chain and motioned me to the gangplank, shaking my hand with a firm grip as he grinned and indicated the pier below with a jerk of his head.

"Your gear's already off," he told me. "Went over the side in one of the nets. Hope to have you as a passenger again sometime, Mister Turk. My pleasure."

I shook my head. "I'm here to stay."

The boy might have been fifteen, but looked less. He was sitting on my saddle there at the foot of the gangplank, seeming to contemplate his big toe with a sense of concentration that cut out the bustle of activity about him. He glanced up in surprise as I paused beside him, then leaped to his feet, grinning broadly. He appeared even smaller in the white cotton shirt and trousers that were several sizes too large and the large, woven frond hat that shaded his dark Polynesian features.

"Mister Turk?" He didn't wait for acknowledgment, but rushed on as though reciting a well-rehearsed speech. "I am Kimo. I am to take you to the ranch."

The simplicity with which he uttered the words told that he was trying to keep the accent from creeping over his voice while he displayed his knowledge of mission-school English.

"I was sent to bring you. I have a wagon waiting."

"How did you know who I was?" The black shape of the other ship was hidden behind one of the warehouses built out onto the wharf, but the tense emptiness still gripped my stomach. He showed surprise again, looking up at me out of liquid-brown eyes as he motioned to where he had been sitting.

"The saddle. A Texas saddle. I was told to look for the man who had it."

I had bought the secondhand saddle and a fast horse in Santa Fe, rousing a liveryman out of his bed to make the purchase. I had been running again.

As I started to reach for the rig, Kimo stepped in ahead of me to raise it to his shoulder, the stirrups almost dragging the ground. As he turned away, he motioned toward the light spring wagon and a team of undersized bays that stood in the dirt street at the end of the wharf.

As we drove through the town the boy was silent, offering me the chance to look it over. It was like others I'd seen—rough and new in some spots, old and stately in others, but it still was a frontier town even two thousand miles from the California Coast. The new buildings of rough lumber going up among the older structures with thatch roofs suggested a new, undeveloped civilization slowly enveloping an older one that had started to decay at the edges.

I suppose that, by that spring, most of the people in the world knew there was a place called Hawaii, but knew little about it. The people moving along the streets I had seen before in the Apache races. They were straight-backed and carried their heads with a stately, dangerous pride.

Unlike the Apaches, though, many of these people smiled and waved to the boy on the seat beside me. He would return the salute, calling to some of them in his best English, which was on display for my benefit, but more often returning a greeting in smooth-flowing Hawaiian syllables that reminded me of water flowing over stones in a stream bed.

The road—a rutted trail cut into the volcanic rock and thin soil by weather and the grinding of steel rims—followed the beach as we left the town. Palm trees stood singly and in groves along the water's edge, giving way to thick jungle underbrush and tall, stately banyan trees with widespread limbs as the ground sloped upward toward the volcanic peaks.

Kimo oriented me, pointing out the distant blue peaks of Mauna Kea, the mountain I had noticed from the ship, and of Mauna Loa, still active as a volcano, which he described as *"kahunu* mountain. Bad." He nodded his head vigorously at his own serious wisdom, adding, "When fire come out, everything burn."

He was silent for a moment, glancing at me shyly from

beneath the brim of his floppy hat, before asking, "What kind of place Texas, Mister Turk? How like this place?"

Some of the formality had gone out of his earlier, carefully phrased English to be replaced by the gutturals of pidgin.

"Mark Hollman's a Texan. If he never told you about it, he's different from any other Texan I've ever known."

A frown of doubt coated his thin features as he shook his head solemnly. "Mister Hollman make little Texas talk. Always this place, cows and *lios*."

"'*Lios*'? What's that?"

"Hawaiian word. Means 'wild-eye.' Means 'horse,' too."

"How'd a horse get a name like that?"

He shook his head, shrugging his lack of knowledge. "Don't know. Just word. Lots of horses in Texas place? What kind of country?"

"I guess it's a lot like this, Kimo. No volcano, no palm trees, but the grass is just as green, I reckon."

The boy turned to look at me with a scowl, pausing before he asked in halting words, "Why you come here, Mister Turk? You no like Texas? You got big *pilikia*, big trouble, like Mister Hollman say?"

I didn't know how to answer. How do you explain to a kid who hardly speaks English that you left because you were afraid? Because someone was trying to kill you?

How did you tell about the shot in the dark in Amarillo and how you had been on the night stagecoach an hour later? How you had packed all of your new hopes into a suitcase with an old Peacemaker and a few clothes, leaving everything else behind tainted with fear?

And how did you explain the rumor in Santa Fe that a man had ridden into town asking for you, then had disappeared before you learned his name or what he wanted? How you had bought a horse and started riding until you hit San Francisco? How the whole thing happened again there only a few weeks later?

Could you explain to him that you were running from a

man you didn't know—had never seen—but who still was a man with a gun? A man who meant to kill you, even though you didn't know why? An explanation deals with tangibles—things that can be understood, or reached for and touched with the fingers.

There was no explanation. None at all that couldn't be capsuled in the single word: Fear!

Two

We drove along the water, halting at what Kimo called "Black Sands" long enough for him to climb a palm tree and twist a pair of green coconuts from their tough stems.

I sat watching as he expertly stripped off the outer husks and punched holes in the brittle shell so that we could drink the chalky-looking milk. When the sweet-tasting nectar had been drained, the Hawaiian boy pounded the shells on the steel wagon rim until they shattered and we could pick out the thick, juicy meat clinging to the sides.

There was something almost grotesque about the beauty of the stretch of beach. As far as I could see, the sands that washed up from the water were black with a stark, unreal quality that left me with an unexplained uneasiness. Palm trees arched their thick trunks toward the sky without sign of concern over the unlikely soil that nurtured their roots. Kimo saw me looking and nodded toward the white surf that washed up over the wide ribbon of black as though to cleanse it.

"Volcano sand," he explained through a mouthful of coconut. "Lava from *kahunu* mountain come down, then water turn into all-black sand."

As we drove on, I saw scattered houses much like those we had left behind in Hilo. Some were simple frame structures, with newness still showing through thin coats of paint. Others were constructed of native timbers and thatched with palm leaves. They seemed to have an aloof appearance, as though not fully approving of the progress that was crowding in about them.

As Kimo swung the team of undersized bays away from the beach, starting upland, the trail narrowed, flanked tight on each side by a thick growth of thorn-bearing keawe trees. When I questioned him about the location of the ranch, he nodded toward the blue-shaded volcano ahead.

"How can you raise cattle up there? It's nothing but rocks!"

My tone was harsh and impatient, but he ignored it as he answered simply, "Not that far."

He pointed to the smaller mountain closer to us, its flat top nearly invisible in the shadows of Mauna Loa. "Ranch near Kilauea, the little mountain."

He glanced at the sun, frowning, and slapped the team with the reins, raising them to a slow, lazy trot. As we bounced along the trail, the steel tires grating noisily in the time-deepened ruts, we both were silent.

The morose expanse of black volcanic sand, with the scattered palms growing up from it, had done something to my mood. It was suddenly as black as the shattered bits of lava that made up the beach. I was angry. Angry with myself. With Mark Hollman. With the little gray man, the warden back at Huntsville.

Hollman had run in the beginning. I had stayed to fight. My reward had been twenty years behind the high, gray walls of the prison and words of wisdom from the little man who made a living telling us how to lead our lives, then went to his home outside the gate each night to think of other things, while we huddled in our stink-filled cells to remember his words and the curses of his guards.

But Hollman hadn't been among us. With the first sign of the range war, he had pulled stakes, salvaging what he could and leaving Texas behind. Now he was manager of one of the largest Hawaiian ranches. For him, running had been smart. Now I was trying to follow the same course, running to leave trouble in my wake. But I was twenty years too late!

The sun was fighting a losing battle with the shadows of the mountains as we dropped into the small, grass-filled valley at the foot of the mountain Kimo had called "Kilauea."

The ranch house was a long, low structure of rough native lumber. Most of the thick logs forming its walls had been squared by hand. Unpainted, it had been turned a deep rustic brown by the weathering of years. The greater part of the roof was of palm-leaf thatch, although one section boasted a layer of newer wooden shakes. Several of the windows in this wing boasted glass panes, while the rest were covered by thin roll blinds fashioned of split bamboo.

Behind the house a section of a corral, most of it constructed of thick bamboo poles, was visible. Beyond was another low building that I took to be the bunkhouse for the hands.

Two riders loped in from the direction of the volcano, which towered several miles away, and pulled up at the corral, swinging down and starting to strip saddles from the backs of their mounts. Both of the animals were small and wiry-looking like Indian mustangs, and one of them bore the white splotches of a pinto.

"Where do you get your horses?" I asked.

Kimo looked at me in surprise at the question. They were the first words that had passed between us in nearly an hour. He had attempted to carry on a conversation as we swung away from the beach of the black sands, but eventually had been affected by my own dark mood and had dropped the effort.

"Born here," he replied. "They ours."

"You never imported any stock from the mainland?"

The boy shrugged, frowning. "Not for many years. What reason? A stallion came from San Francisco when I was a small child. That was the last. Are they not good horses?"

The formality was back in his voice, and I wondered whether I had offended him as he indicated the team before us. As he pulled up the wagon, the horses lowered their heads wearily, but despite the long, uphill pull, their flanks were barely rising. Kimo leaped down and started to take my bag from the back of the wagon.

"Not here. You'd better put it in the bunkhouse," I told him. He hesitated, glancing toward the house, then nodded and went to the team to lead them across the open area.

Doubt flooded over my other thoughts as I stood watching him for a moment, then turned to the heavy koa-wood door.

It was like meeting an old girl friend who has drifted away and married someone else. It was nearly twenty years since I had last seen Mark Hollman. Nineteen years, two months, to be exact. Friendships don't last that long unless they're cultivated to keep the weeds of time and distance from engulfing them and leaving only withered memories.

My knock on the smooth, polished panel was answered by a short, graying woman with seamed features and the dark, piercing eyes of a Japanese. When I told her my name and that I was expected, she only nodded and turned to lead me down a long, dark hallway that led to the far wing of the house.

The structure was unlike any I had ever been in before. The walls were of hand-hewn native lumber and decorated with rugs and a stiff cloth that, I later found out, was called *tapa*, which was made from the bark of trees, then decorated with hand-blocked symbols. At intervals, coconuts—the thick husks carved to form grotesque pagan faces—decorated the walls. Crude spears and heavy, notched war clubs hung between the expanses of cloth, too.

There was something eerie about the place, almost ghostlike. As I followed the silent Oriental over the heavy woven mats that covered the floor, I felt a vain attempt to hold onto the past, to block progress by throwing in its path this collection of pagan art. It was the mark of a stubborn man trying to protect himself against the future by dwelling on a dream of past greatness.

But Mark Hollman didn't bear out these thoughts. He rose from behind a huge teakwood desk and came forward, while the Japanese woman silently closed the door behind me.

Neither of us said anything for a moment as we stared into each other's faces. Mark Hollman was a man of thirty the last time I had seen him. I was ten years younger. But before me now I saw a man who had grown heavy with responsibility. Heavy in body and features. And heavy in thought.

He wore a khaki-colored shirt open at the throat, and levis that had been washed nearly white, the normal, dark-blue color clinging only around the stitching of the seams. The cloth was tight across his barrel chest, and his stomach protruded over his thick leather belt like a boulder at the edge of a cliff, needing only a strong wind to send it crashing down.

His face was burned a deep brown, and his once brown hair was showing gray at the temples, while the tropical sun had bleached the longer growth in blond, uneven streaks. There were wrinkles about his eyes that belonged to an older man, and the weight of responsibility had pulled his mouth down at the corners to give him an expression of sorrow.

Only his eyes were the same. They were a deep, unreadable purple—between blue and black—and reflected the blanket of reserve that was held up for me to see and accept in spite of his outstretched hand.

"Glad to see you, Sam," he said quietly. "Been a long time."

"Twenty years, less time off for good behavior."

He looked up at me quickly, eyes narrowing to a frown as he shook his head. "That wasn't what I meant, Sam. Sit down."

I took the chair beside his desk as he moved around the teakwood bulk and lowered himself into the creaking swivel chair, still frowning. There were things he wanted to say but he wasn't certain where to start, what to say first. He pretended to look over some of the papers before him for a moment, and I couldn't help seeing that the one on top was the letter I had written him from San Francisco.

"Why'd you come here, Sam? You need a job, sure, and maybe someone's been trying to bushwhack you, like you said in your letter, but why here? What's it all about?" He kept his tone guarded, but it wasn't defensive. It was more as though he wanted to protect my feelings, didn't want to push me into answering something I didn't want to.

"It was all in the letter. I'm on the run, and have been ever since I walked through those iron gates at Huntsville. First it was in Amarillo. Someone tried to gun me in the dark. Then Santa Fe. Someone showed up asking questions about where to find Sam Turk. I didn't stay long enough to find out who he was or what he looked like, but it all happened again in Frisco, while I was waiting to hear from you."

It was a long speech, and he sat nodding his understanding as I spewed the words at him. But his expression didn't change. The frown was a stepchild of apprehension, of worry.

"This is a peaceful country, Sam," Mark Hollman declared thoughtfully after a moment's hesitation. "You have to understand that. It's not like Texas was. It's good cattle country, and a man can make a good thing here. I didn't send for you out of pity or even for old-time's sake. I need good men, but not if they have a chip on their shoulders."

I nodded. "Maybe you picked the wrong man, Mark. It's been a long time. You can forget things you learned when you've spent the last twenty years with nothing to do at night but walk six feet to a wall, then walk six feet back."

"I hope to God you have forgotten *some* things!" There was a touch of harshness in his tone that grew as he went on.

"This is no country for guns, Turk. The only weapon I own is up there on the wall. None of my men are allowed to carry a weapon except maybe a knife!"

I glanced up at the carbine that hung from the two pegs driven into the log wall behind his head. He had carried the same weapon in his saddle scabbard the day he rode out of Jefferson for the last time, leaving me standing there in the lonely, dusty street.

"I'm here to work," I told him simply. "You know all about the past, Mark, but I'd like to leave it behind me. Standing back there on a pier in San Francisco."

He was looking down at my letter which still lay before him, and his frown worked its way into a full-fledged scowl.

"You should have left Texas when I did," he growled. "But someone convinced you you were fighting for right and that your gun could help. There's never a right or wrong in a cattle war, and both sides end up losing. You lost, didn't you? Twenty years of your life is a lot to gamble for right. Even with time off for good behavior!"

"You weren't there, Mark. They hired a gunslinger and it was self-defense. Me or him."

"I didn't have to be there. I'd seen it before. That's why I wanted no part of it." He was nodding at me thoughtfully, his voice low but tense. "Two men in the middle of a dusty street, each with a gun in his hand to prove his side is right. That picture doesn't change. You were the better man, sure. But what about that other man? The general-store man that got killed? And the kid that got shot? Can you call that self-defense, Sam?" His tone was rough with bitterness and accusation.

It had been a long time since anger had worked its way up through my throat. Anger had gotten me thirty days in a black, stinking hole once. After a while, I had learned to forget the sensation. Now anger was a strange, almost wild thing that I fought to force back.

"They were wild bullets, and they never proved they

came from my gun. But I paid for it, remember? Man-slaughter!"

As he looked up at me then, I realized suddenly that Mark Hollman was an old man. It was as though he had been wearing his scowl to disguise this fact. Now, with it gone, age crept through his pores to blanket his features. He shook his head slowly.

"Like you say, Sam, I left before most of it happened. All I know is that I don't want any trouble. And that's something that's always rode on your shoulder. As far as I'm concerned, your past is dead. No one here will know about it." He turned his eyes to the side of the room, staring at a painting. "These islands have been good to me. They gave me a wife, a child and responsibility. I don't want any trouble this late in the game."

The painting was old and the canvas was starting to crack beneath the colors, but there still was a beauty about the subject that held my eyes. She had been Hawaiian with dark skin, bright, black eyes and full lips. Her hair appeared thick and black, seeming to form a halo about her head as she stared down with a haughty, still, soft air.

"My wife," Mark said simply. "She's been dead almost eighteen years."

I settled back in the chair, the tenseness born of my anger dissolving. "What about the ranch? How many head of cattle do you run? What do I have to know to go to work?"

"Right now we're running about ten thousand head. Steers, heifers and cows. The owners are in England and have never been here." A cynical smile came into his eyes as he continued. "Started by one of the old missionary families who, as the natives put it, came here to do good and did well."

The ring of steel on rock came through the window, and Hollman paused, listening, then looked back to me. The view of the trail leading up to the house was cut off by the heavy shrubs.

"That must be Malia. She rode into Hilo with Kimo this morning. I expected her back before this. Must have had some trouble finding the bookkeeper I had coming in," he explained as he rose from behind the desk and moved toward the door to the hallway, indicating with a wave that I should follow him.

There were three men with the girl, but it was she who held my attention. She wore a dark buckskin riding skirt that must have been ordered from the mainland. Gray in color, it matched her broadcloth shirt that was open at the throat. She wore no hat, and her thick, black hair hung below the level of her shoulders, forming a frame for olive-toned features that betrayed her Hawaiian blood. It was not difficult to see the close resemblance to the woman I had seen in the cracked painting in Hollman's office.

Her eyes were as dark as her hair, and her parted, smiling lips showed me white, even teeth made even brighter by the contrast with her dark face. She could have been no more than eighteen, but looked older. The tightness of the gray fabric across the full round of her breasts added to the look of maturity. She glanced at me curiously, then turned her attention to Hollman.

"I found your new man, Father. He was wandering through the streets not certain that he had come to the right place at all." She was laughing as she glanced at one of the men and he stepped forward to exchange grips with the ranch manager.

"Stuart Himmler? I'm Mark Hollman. Welcome and *aloha.*"

The man called Himmler nodded with a smile, saying, "Thank you, sir, but there are a couple of others here who wanted to meet you."

The other two, who had been standing by their horses, came forward, halting before Hollman for his inspection, almost as though it were a ritual.

Himmler was tall and angular, with thick-lensed spectacles that caused his eyes to seem out of proportion with the rest of his red, sunburned face. He wore a shiny suit of black broadcloth, a rumpled shirt with a yellowed celluloid collar and a string tie that had seen better days. His shoes were cracked with age beneath their new coat of polish, and there was the red rust of age on the black felt hat he carried beneath his arm. He might have been forty. Or sixty. The only hint of age were the gray streaks edging up over his ears from each temple to cut into his jet-colored hair.

The second man was dressed in a flannel shirt open at the neck to show brown chest hair topping a barrel-shaped torso set on thin, bowed legs encased in faded levis. His hair was long and stringy, and there was a stubble of red-blond beard on his grinning face. But it was his eyes that sent a warning ripple telegraphing along my spine. They were light blue and devoid of any sign of pleasure or amusement. I'd seen eyes like his before. A whole prisonful. Gunfighter's eyes. And there was a worn spot on the right leg of his trousers, where a holster might have rubbed. Below it a thin, blue band about his leg was not as faded as the rest of the fabric. A gun artist who favored a tiedown gun.

The last man was younger than the others. Twenty-five. No more. He wore a gray business suit and carried a flat-crowned hat, and peeking from beneath the carefully pressed trousers were high-heeled cowman's boots. His black, tightly combed hair might have been curly if he had allowed it, while his face, brown and handsome in its boyish-ness, made more pronounced a delicately arched nose and brown eyes of the type that reflect sorrow, worry or trouble too easily. But his right cheek was marred by a deep scar that ran upward to explain the nick in his ear lobe. His eyes were on the girl as the man named Himmler introduced them.

"These two are looking for work," he explained. "Your daughter didn't know what to tell them, so she brought them along at my suggestion."

The gunman, still grinning, stepped forward to face Holl-man with an arrogance born of confidence.

"I'm Jeff Slack," he announced shortly. "Punched a lot of cows and know the business."

Mark nodded without speaking, but turned his glance to the younger man inquisitively.

"Drake Martin," was the quiet self-introduction. "I know something about cows, too."

"All three of us came over on the *Black Star*," Himmler offered for Hollman's benefit.

The rancher's eyes turned to me and he was making introductions that I hardly heard. I nodded automatically as I studied the faces of the three, searching for something even I couldn't identify. A sign. A reason. A memory. These three had arrived on the ship that left San Francisco the day after I had sailed. Fear was crawling in my stomach like a blacksnake after a cornered mouse, and I could feel the muscles of my face tighten with sudden strain.

One of these three had come to kill me!

But which one?

And why?

Three

In 1794, Captain George Vancouver, representing the British Crown, sailed into a now forgotten inlet on the island of Hawaii and unloaded several head of cattle, which had been presented to the Hawaiian King, Kamehameha, as a gift of friendship.

The monarch, proud of these new oddities, posted warnings that they were *kapu*—forbidden—to all except his own family. In those days the royal family held the power of life and death over all in the Islands. To break a *kapu* was considered automatic death.

Several years later, Captain Richard J. Cleveland, another British seaman, anchored off a spot known as Kawaihae and sent ashore a mare and her foal as a similar gesture toward the royal family. If the Hawaiian ruler suspected the sea captains were taking part in a plan to build an English colony in his domain—as later proved true—he ignored it and accepted the gifts.

The mare, which had been shipped from California, was so frightened as a result of the rough passage and the treatment by her inexperienced handlers that, according to legend, she lashed out at everyone who came close to her offspring.

Several natives who had helped with the unloading went away nursing broken bones as the mare and colt finally swam ashore and disappeared into the jungle.

The wild rolling of the animal's eyes and screams of fear and anger had earned her a name—*lio*—meaning "wild-eyed," as Kimo had told me the first morning. All other horses born in the Islands became known by the same term.

The Hawaiian cattle industry came later, after a young Massachusetts sailor named John Parker found himself sailing the Pacific islands aboard an English merchant ship as the War of 1812 flared.

The news of hostilities between England and the United States brought an abrupt change in the attitude of his British shipmates, and when the ship paused at Kohala to take aboard food and water, John Parker deserted. He stayed hidden in the jungles until the skipper tired of searching for him, ordered the crew back aboard and sailed away.

At first, John Parker attempted to make a living from truck farming, selling his scanty crops to passing ships. It took little time for him to discover that most were as interested in provisioning their larders with beef as with his produce.

Parker approached Kamehameha III and was granted the sole right of shooting cattle, butchering them and selling the meat to trading vessels.

During this time, some of the Hawaiians had sufficiently recovered from the fear instilled by the wild mare, whose offspring now thronged the Island. The Islanders made a sport of capturing the *lios* and trying to ride them.

Kamehameha eventually sent a member of the royal family to California as an ambassador of good will and soon received word that the horsemanship of the Spanish *vaqueros* was a thing of wonderment. At the monarch's insistence, several Spaniards and Mexicans soon arrived to teach his people how to ride, break horses and handle cattle on a commercial basis.

"We had a going cattle industry here before Crockett and Bowie ever heard of the Alamo," Hollman told me one day shortly after I arrived. "While your pappy and mine was still beatin' off Injuns, the Parkers and some of the rest was in business."

It was out of this series of incidents that Hawaii's cattle ranches developed. According to the story, the early Spanish riders told the Islanders they were *Español*. The natives immediately associated the word with anyone who was a fine horseman. The word *"paniolo,"* Hawaiian for "cowboy," became a part of the native language, as a corruption of the Spanish.

Some of this I learned from Hollman, some came from Kimo in his carefully voiced mission-school English. The rest I had learned from Malia the day I mentioned that most of the saddles and even the rawhide riatas were of Spanish origin and design.

In the weeks that followed, I learned about the ranch. At first I stuck close to the headquarters, working with the horse wranglers. I talked about riding once or twice, but Hollman shook his head. He didn't give a reason for his refusal, but it wasn't hard to figure. I hadn't been on a bucking horse since before the range war. I was too old to start over at that game. Too far gone.

With Kimo, I rode over the range, learning the location of water holes and checking the grasslands that stretched up to the rough lava expanses marking the beginning of the volcano.

The Hawaiian boy seemed afraid of the black towering peak, but said nothing even when we rode partway up the slope one afternoon, following a tortuous trail through the rough, glass-edged lava formations. It was Hollman who told me the reason for his fears, when I mentioned them.

"He used to ride up there a lot," Mark explained that evening as we sat on the *lanai,* watching the sun drop behind the peak. "He and a couple of the other kids was playing up there the day she broke loose." He paused, frowning into the bowl of his pipe, and I waited for him to go on.

"She erupted. That mountain's guts started growling,

and all at once she was throwin' lava all over the place. Almost got the kids. That's why I'm responsible for Kimo. His old man was killed when he went ridin' up there to look for them. Got caught in the lava. Used to be one of my best riders."

There was little I could do except nod my understanding. And I realized a little more of the responsibility that hung so heavily on Hollman's shoulders.

At times, Mark and Malia would ride over the ranch with me, indoctrinating me in what he called "the little man's Texas," explaining the markers showing where this ranch ended and the huge expanse of the Parker ranch began.

"Biggest ranch here, the Parkers have. Real nice people. Right helpful and law-abiding," Mark declared one afternoon as we sat our horses on a low rise overlooking one of the neighboring ranch's herds.

The Parker cattle looked heavier, carried more meat than the gaunt, stringy Island cattle I'd seen before. Here and there a calf showed the telltale white head and stockings of the Hereford strain. New blood was being introduced.

"Most of the people around here are law-abiding," Hollman went on slowly. "Somebody may steal a cow every now and then for the meat, but it don't pose much of a problem. It's one of the things we expect, and we don't make no trouble over it."

I knew the words were meant for me, but I ignored them.

Malia, riding with us, was staring at me thoughtfully when I glanced in her direction. She turned away to look at the cattle, a little frown flitting across her features. I found myself wondering how much she knew about me. About my past. Then I swore silently for caring. She wasn't twenty. I was nearly twice that.

Most of the time the girl was shy and distant and said little even when we both were in the company of her father. There was a quiet pride about the way she carried herself, whether wearing her customary riding costume of a man's faded shirt, rough, knee-high boots and a leather riding skirt, or whether she was dressed in one of the sacklike Mother Hubbards introduced by the early missionaries as a futile cure for the passions that Island women seem to inspire in visiting seamen.

She was tall, touching five feet six or seven, with a back that was as straight as a reformer's promise. Even beneath the billowing material of the old shirt she wore when riding, her well-formed breasts continually announced their presence, outlining their gentle curves beneath the cloth whenever a breeze drew the material against her figure or she would move quickly.

When riding, she piled her shoulder-length hair atop her head in a bun and hid it beneath her hat, looking like a teenage boy trying to convince himself he was a man. Loose, with the dark sheen trailing behind her, its blackness reflected the light with the brilliance born of daily care.

Though many Hawaiian women are inclined to grow heavy in later years as a result of lazy living, good food and bearing too many children, there was no sign that this would happen to Malia.

Her mother had been Hawaiian and an offspring of the royal family, where women's virtues were counted in the number of children they could bear and their degree of beefy weight, which often hit three hundred pounds. But she had that lithe grace that was evident even in the form of a sleeping cat.

Sometimes, when watching her with Hollman, it was hard to believe that she actually could be his daughter, the product of his seed. As a young man, Mark had been thin and nervous, always on the move, looking for a better life. Now he had developed a squat steadiness, emphasized by the protrusion of his stomach over his belt buckle. He moved slowly and allowed his thoughts to follow only one channel —making money for the ranch's British owners.

Malia had few of his features, having inherited the beauty

I had noticed in the painting of Mark's wife which hung in his office. Her forehead was just a little too high before it met her black hair, a trait with most Polynesians. But this went unnoticed once you looked into her eyes, which were shaded by long lashes inclined to curl up at the ends.

But somewhere back in the dark depths of her eyes was a smoldering fire marking the passion of her Island ancestry. Several times, when I had caught her looking at me as though I was unaware, I had seen that fire smoldering near the surface and had caught my blood quickening, then had ended up cursing myself for thinking about it.

She seldom spoke to the ranch workers other than Kimo, who seemed to hold an unspoken bond with her, but the others treated her with a deference which I laid to the royal blood in her veins. In time, I realized there was a note of tragedy somewhere in her quiet way and want of a smile.

I wondered how much genuine affection she had received from Mark during her early years. He was always gentle with her, allowing her to do much as she wished, but there was an invisible wall between them most of the time. It might have had to do with the fact that her mother had died in childbirth, I reasoned. But it was none of my business.

It was none of my business, either, that Hollman announced a holiday for a *hukilau* and that, during the community fishing and festivities that followed, the girl sat showing Drake Martin how to play the ukulele and smiling at him. Mark pretended not to be watching, but a scowl played tag with the corners of his mouth each time the young man with the scarred cheek and the girl joined in bursts of laughter over his clumsiness in fingering the strings.

Or maybe it was Martin's nearness to the girl, who wore nothing but a short sarong and seemed to revel in its briefness after coming out of the lagoon with thin cloth plastered to her body. It was as though donning the sarong was like shedding a skin that was old and torn and that she was starting a new kind of life. It was the birth—or rebirth—of a pagan!

We had come down to the lagoon early in the day, most riding, while the married men drove wagons with their women, children and yards upon yards of fishing nets. All had been waiting for the affair for weeks, and there was a great deal of banter back and forth, with children shrieking their expectations.

Malia had ridden with her father, a hibiscus blossom tucked over her left ear to express the spirit of festivity—and to signify that she was unmarried and available. A flower over the other ear, I learned, meant that one was either married or spoken for.

It was the flower that first caused Mark's frown. He kept eying the blossom as he rode toward the beach, but said nothing to her as he explained the *hukilau* to me.

According to Hollman's explanation, the affair began as a simple means of survival, with all of the occupants of an Island village turning out to aid in dropping the long nets around a school of fish, then dragging them in with the catch. Once the catch was made, the fish were divided according to the size of each family which had taken part.

As Mark and I sat with our backs against one of the palm trees that edged the narrow expanse of beach, the Hawaiian men and women were dragging the net from the water, the back muscles of the nearly bare men glinting a shiny bronze beneath the reflective coatings of sweat. There were constant laughter and exchanges in Hawaiian, Japanese, Chinese, Portuguese and pidgin English as the children waded close to the net, trying to push each other into its heavy folds as an added bit of sport. Even from where I sat, I caught the silver gleam of scaled forms flopping about frantically as the net was hauled laboriously from deep water to the foam-capped surf.

Kimo and Ben Low, Hollman's top wrangler, were standing on a point of rock away from the others, looking down into the deeper waters of the lagoon. Each wore only a patterned loincloth which had been bleached by past exposures to salt and sun. Each had a tight-woven circular net with weighted edges slung across his shoulders.

As I watched, Kimo, then Low, hurled the nets out over the water, the pull of the stone weights spreading each into a perfect circle of mesh. Both retained light lines attached to the nets, and I heard Kimo's excited shout, followed by Ben Low's deep-throated laughter, as they started to pull in their catches.

Hollman, still wearing boots and tight-fitting riding pants, had removed his shirt and sat with his back to the palm. He puffed at his pipe solemnly, watching a small lizard that had crept from the thick brush to our rear and was now crawling cautiously before us, leaving a tiny trail in the sand with its overlong tail.

He looked up quickly as the tinkle of Malia's light laughter came to us. She handed the ukulele to Drake Martin again, still laughing as she said, "Go ahead. It is not at all difficult." Her words had the musical upbeat at the end peculiar to pidgin. The slight accent was there in spite of the fact that her enunciation was school-perfect.

Martin wore an old pair of trousers which he had torn off at the knees. They were now white with sand, which had stuck to their wetness after he had come in with Malia from helping with the *hukilau* net. He took the instrument but shook his head, glancing at the girl with a grin. There was something shy—almost bashful—about his expression.

"My mother spent half the family fortune on music lessons for me before my father died," he told her. "None of it ever stuck for long."

"Never mind, then," she half scolded. "I shall teach you myself. Put your fingers where I tell you."

The girl moved closer across the sand, until her hip rested against his, and reached out to place the young man's fingers on the frets of the handmade instrument. She said something that didn't carry to where we were sitting, but Drake Martin laughed uneasily, looking away from her as his blond chest hair quivered in the sunlight. With his heavy coating of tan, part of which I knew he must have cultivated en route from Frisco aboard the ship, he reminded me of a young bull just beginning to realize his useful purpose in life.

I was wondering whether Martin had noticed that strange something far back in the girl's dark eyes, as Hollman muttered something under his breath. He was scowling as I swung my eyes toward him, and the expression grew no less tense when he saw that I was watching, too.

"Something I've been wanting to talk to you about, Sam," Hollman said dourly. "This operation's getting to be pretty big now. Too big for me to oversee by myself. I've been tied up with book work more than I've been checking the range."

"Yeah?"

He hesitated, glancing toward his daughter and the blond giant, going ahead as he watched Martin's clumsy efforts at drawing music from the strings of the ukulele.

"Ben's been talking some about quitting. Has some fool idea about going to the States and seeing what the cattle business is like there. He decides to pull up stakes, I'm going to need a foreman."

Malia laughed again, and Hollman glanced toward her with visible annoyance before turning back to me.

"You reckon you could handle the job and keep out of trouble?"

"I might, if you'd be willing to let me be a ramrod and not a whipping boy," I told him.

"Maybe I rode you some when you first come, Sam, but I reckon you wouldn't blame me much for that," Hollman said with slow, measured words. "I kept remembering you the way you used to be, always hot-tempered and looking for trouble."

"I learned one thing the hard way down there at Huntsville, Mark. You don't have to look for trouble. It's always around. What's a lot harder to find is a way of keeping way clear of it."

He nodded. "I know. I've been watching you, Sam, but sometimes you still get that funny look in your eye. Like you used to get when you was expecting big trouble to pop. Anything really bothering you now?"

I was looking toward Stuart Himmler, his figure thin, gaunt and ridiculous in the rusty suit and white shirt, as he stood near the water's edge, staring out through the opening that led from the lagoon to the open sea. He stood perfectly motionless, hands clasped behind his back, while he stared into a thought that was a million miles long.

"We can talk about it later," I said. "Ben hasn't quit yet."

"Yeah. You're right on that." He was following my gaze. "What about *him*, Mark? Where'd he come from?"

"Somewhere in the East. He's a good bookkeeper."

Although I had tried to make my question sound casual, disinterested, Hollman's answer held rebuke in its tone, as though to say this was a question that should never be asked. He pulled his feet up beneath him, starting to rise.

"Just remembered. Got to remind him about a report that we've got to get out on the boat for London tomorrow morning."

For a moment, my temper had started to flare at the tone he used in answering me. Then I remembered. He hadn't told anyone about my past. Maybe the bookkeeper preferred it that way, too.

Himmler turned to face Mark as he paused beside him at the water's edge. Even in the bright sunlight his face looked gray and tired. Most of his initial sunburn had faded from his daily work over the account ledgers. His eyes were big and unreal behind the thick lenses of his spectacles as he stood listening intently to Hollman, nodding his understanding.

Himmler seemed to be speaking freely enough now, but I hadn't heard him say a dozen words since the evening he arrived at the ranch with Martin and Slack. While the two riders and I had been assigned space in the bunkhouse, he had been moved into a room in the main building. He appeared to be a man married to a column of figures, tied to the ledgers and account books by a continual stream of reports to England, telling the owners the margins of profit or what could be expected.

I rarely saw him outside the house during the day, and on several occasions when I'd gone into Mark's office at night on business, he would be bending over the official-looking volumes piled high before him, fingers stained with ink, hair rumpled. The most he had ever offered when I asked for Hollman and where he could be found was a noncommittal shrug, not looking up from his work. Now, as he and Mark stood with their backs toward me, looking out to sea, I saw that same shrug. A silent man, someone had told me once, can be the most dangerous. As I sat looking, I wondered about Himmler. How long had he been silent?

A stick cracked behind me and I turned to look around the trunk of the tree to the jungle, which grew down to the high-tide line. Jeff Slack stood there, a hand-rolled cigarette dangling from the corner of his mouth. It was the first time I had seen him since we had left the main ranch. He was dressed in the same faded blue denims bearing the gun marks I'd noticed that first evening. His work shirt and the inner part of the brim of his hat were wet with the same sweat that blanketed his face.

As he stood looking toward Malia and Drake Martin, who were laughing at some private joke, he failed to see me. At the sound from the girl, his face twisted into a hard, hawkish expression, the lips dangling the cigarette tightening into a tight, black line. His stance was that of a mountain lion about to charge a motherless colt, but it was his eyes that bothered me most. They were cold in their blueness and unblinking. Gunman's eyes, I had thought when I first saw them. I'd seen a lot of men with those eyes behind those high, gray walls at Huntsville.

They had that same look when they wanted one of two things. When they wanted to kill. And when they wanted a woman!

Four

It was late that night when the caravan returned to the ranch and disbanded, friends and neighbors whispering farewells to avoid waking the children. Most of the families lived in small houses scattered over the ranch, and some had left the group before we arrived at the main head-quarters.

Ben Low, who functioned as foreman as well as Holl-man's top wrangler, Slack and I turned our horses into the corral, and I glanced about for Martin. Riding back, I had heard him tell Malia that he would turn in her mount for her, and Low had already taken care of Hollman's horse. But as I stood waiting, the corral bars still down, I caught no sound of Martin or the other horse.

"If he's out there in the dark with her, you'll probably have to wait all night," Slack volunteered at my shoulder.

As I turned to stare at him, there was nothing visible in the blackness but the red glow of his cigarette coal. But the look I had seen on his face earlier as he stood watching Malia was still in my mind. I said nothing as I put up the bars and turned toward the bunkhouse, leaving him stand-ing there alone. Low had waited for neither of us.

The bulk of the bunkhouse was looming against the stars as I heard the sound of hooves and the creak of saddle leather. I halted beside a broad fern to look back, still seeing the glow of the cigarette. Slack chuckled deep in his throat as Drake Martin pulled up at the corral, and I heard Martin's saddle creak as he swung down and dropped the bars before starting to strip the two horses.

"That gal's real purty-lookin' flesh, Martin," Slack's drawl declared over his chuckle. "A man with a little experience and know-how could be real happy with that."

There was no answer as I heard the slap of the saddles being thrown up to the top pole of the corral. The bridles rattled and clanked, then the two horses snorted as they bolted into the corral.

"They always told me the quiet fellers was the ones making out the greatest," Slack went on in his half-chiding tone. "You really that good or just want me to think so?"

The lazy humor in his drawl caused the nerves in my shoulders to bunch. I started back to the corral, then stopped, still listening.

"Just cut it off right there, Jeff. I don't care for talk like that," Martin muttered in a low tone that I could scarcely hear.

Slack's laugh came again, louder, and there was less of the easy banter in his tone as he said, "Didn't mean no harm, friend. Just tryin' to keep abreast of the times. Kinda like to know which of the women has been tapped."

The slap of leather and the rattle of metal almost combined with the crash of a body against the corral bars. The lone pinpoint of light, Slack's cigarette, arced away in a trail of sparks. As I raced toward them, my eyes became more used to the darkness and I could make out Drake Martin standing with the bridle over his head. He was about to bring the heavy steel bit crashing down on the other's head again as he cursed in slow, guttural tones of anger. There was something almost methodical in his movements.

I grabbed his arm and jerked the bridle away from him just before he brought it lashing down toward Jeff Slack again. Martin whirled on me, his curses gaining force at the interference.

"Get away from me. This is none of your affair!"

I saw the white of his shirt in the blackness and caught the flash of a sleeve as he swung at me. Using one of the reins as a whip, I lashed out, jerking as the leather encircled his wrist. Off balance, he spun about where I could grab his arm and push it into the small of his back in a hammerlock.

Slack suddenly was on his feet, and I could hear his gasps of rage forcing their way between his clenched teeth as he moved in on us.

"I'll kill you for that!" he snarled. I released my hold on Martin to spin him behind me and stand between them.

"Hold it, Slack!" I snapped the words at him with a viciousness I didn't feel, but they had their effect. He stopped, legs spread wide, listening in surprise. "I don't know what this is all about and I don't want to know, but you'd both better forget it as of now. Hollman won't stand for any trouble. He'll fire you if he hears about this."

"But he was making talk about—" Drake's voice was high-pitched with wrath, almost a whine.

"Shut up! I said I don't want to know. That much of it, at least, is none of my affair, but I know that neither one of you has enough money to book passage even as far as Honolulu. If you want to go on battling and then draw your pay, Mark Hollman won't mind that."

They both stood there, shoulders heaving heavily, dim outlines in the night. Finally, Jeff Slack stooped to recover his hat and strode past us toward the bunkhouse. He paused several steps away.

"Tell me something, Turk." His voice was quiet now, as though trouble was the farthest thing from his mind. "Have you ever been in Texas?"

Suddenly the chill of fear was with me and I tried to look into the darkness, to see his every move, but all he did was turn and walk toward the low outline of the building, where lights were burning in the windows. He knew. He knew about me. The past.

"What's he mean by that?" Martin asked at my shoulder. I turned back to him, my voice more harsh than I meant it to be.

"Better keep all this quiet. Hollman don't like this kind of ruckus. Talk gets out about it, you and Slack'll both find yourselves combing beaches for enough to eat."

"He was askin' for it," he growled. "The things he said I wouldn't—"

"Just take my advice, kid. Forget it, and I will." I paused, wondering how far I should go. The sudden poison of fear coursing through my veins like the bite of a rattlesnake had made me wary.

"But I thought you and Slack was partners. The way you was vouchin' for each other when you turned up here after work, one'd of thought you'd been sharin' the same saddle most of your lives."

"Like hell! Never even seen each other till we was aboard that ship coming out of Frisco. Know him as well now as I ever want to!"

I put my hand on the younger man's shoulder and pushed him gently toward the bunkhouse. He brushed it away, still angry and unsettled.

"Might as well get used to sleepin' under the same roof," I told him. "You can't just stand out here growling at the stars the rest of the night, no matter what he said." I turned to walk away, while he followed.

Lanterns hung from ceiling rafters threw their smoky yellow light over the interior of the two-room structure. The larger section was the bunkhouse proper, while the attached shed at the rear was the cook shack where Joe Tam, the Chinese-Hawaiian cook, turned out meals for the crew.

The Islanders, including Tam and Ben Low, were seated at a table in the middle of the room, laughing over an Oriental card game that was in progress.

Slack had already shed his clothing and was slipping naked into his bunk at the rear of the room. He didn't look up as we entered, but turned his face to the wall and pretended to sleep. His clothing, still yellow with the dust of the corral, hung on a wooden peg above him. If any of the others had noticed the obvious fact that he had been on his back, nothing was said. All were too engrossed in their game of fantan. I paused between Low and another player, and Martin shuffled to the rear of the room, where his bunk stood opposite Slack's.

Drake paused for a moment, staring down at the other man's bare back that showed above the blanket. Finally he shrugged and dropped onto his own rack, noisily pulled off his boots and kicked them beneath the wooden bunk frame.

"Maybeso the game bettah is played in Texas?" Joe Tam wanted to know in pidgin, eying me speculatively in the yellow light that pyramided down upon the table. "Maybeso you hava money, we find out how much good, huh?"

I started to speak, but Ben Low muttered something to him in Chinese and he turned back to the game. But his malicious, sullen scowl didn't go away. I knew the reason for it.

Tam had been present the day I saw Low tie himself into the saddle on one of the ranch's worst horses. Malia had been sitting on the corral fence beside him when I told her that a Texas wrangler would rather shoot himself than be caught pulling such a stunt.

"Perhaps you would be willing to show the poor pagans how a man from Texas rides," she suggested icily, and Tam went into peals of laughter from where he stood behind us.

"I haven't been on a bucking horse for twenty years," I told her, not looking around at the cook.

"My father says that Texas men sometimes make claims they cannot meet," she declared, sliding off the fence to walk toward the house, her back stiff with anger.

It was the most I had ever heard the girl say in one sitting, and I was surprised. Until then, she had clung to the background, apparently satisfied to be overshadowed by her father and expressing no thoughts of her own.

Tam had always seemed friendly enough until I had libeled his friend, Low, but after that he had thrown up an invisible wall and seldom missed a chance to needle me. Some of the other hands of Hawaiian and Chinese extraction had developed the same attitude. Ben Low, if he had heard of the incident, had not changed, though. He had continued, always smiling, always offering a friendly word, as though seeking to make up for the others.

Tam's comment over the poker table now, insulting as it was meant to be, still came as a surprise to me, though. Until now, he had made a definite point of ignoring me since the horse incident. Tam gave his attention to the game, as Low had apparently told him to do, finally glancing up at me once more with his expression of cynical invitation.

I shook my head at him. "Anytime I sit down with the Chinese to play a Chinese game, I want more money than I've got now," I told him. "I did that once back home, and lost a saddle to the boy that usually did my laundry!"

It hadn't actually happened, but the story brought an appreciative chuckle from Low's throat, and some of the belligerence faded out of Joe Tam's eyes as he turned back to the table.

Most professional gamblers are familiar with the version of fantan played with cards in which the banker deals one card to each player and the rest of the deck is placed face down on the table, while the players ante.

Working from the banker's left, the first player is called upon to play an ace. If he has none, he antes into the pot and draws from the deck. The game goes the rounds until one of the players is able to meet the demand for an ace. The following player must then play a king or pay into the pot. Winner is the man who plays off all of his cards first.

But this was the Chinese version, which was introduced

to America during the California gold-rush days by Oriental immigrants. It was later adopted by the professionals of the Barbary Coast and similar places.

A square had been carved into the wooden table top, and its gouged form had long since been worn smooth from nightly play. Ben Low, acting as the croupier, would throw a handful of coins into the square and cover them with his hat before anyone had an opportunity to make a quick count. The sides of the square were designated by numerals, one through four, one side for each of the players who were called upon to place bets. When all stakes were down, Ben would remove the hat and begin pulling coins from the square, four at a time, until four or less coins remained. The number still in the square marked the winner, who collected from the others and gave a minor percentage to Low. If there were four coins remaining, the man playing the number-four position was the winner, and so on with the others.

I watched for a few minutes, then turned to the rear of the room, where my bunk was located. The place was fashioned like most of the bunkhouses I had seen in Texas in other days, but there was a reason for this. Hollman had told me, as he showed me about the ranch, that he had drawn up the plans for it himself less than a week after he had taken over as manager.

On the evening of our arrival, Slack, Martin and myself had been given spare bunks which were ranged along each wall in upper and lower tiers. Mark had told the Japanese housekeeper to ready a room in the main house for Himmler, the bookkeeper.

As I sat on the bunk, pulling off my boots and loosening my shirt, my mind ran over the words I had offered Martin after his fight with Jeff Slack. Since our arrival, neither of the pair had said more than a dozen words to me at a single stretch. Furthermore, I had noticed that they hadn't been talking much to each other either, but still there seemed to be some strange kind of bond between them, something more than the fact that they had arrived on the same ship and had come to the same place to work. The happenings there in the darkness of the corral had dissolved that bond.

Remembering my terror at their sudden appearance at the ranch and the knowledge that they had arrived on the next ship behind me from Frisco, I felt a strange sort of satisfaction. Some of the thoughts that had plagued my brain from the beginning now drifted away into nothing. I feared they were teamed up to get me, even though I knew of no reason. It was their clannish behavior and refusal to talk, but I realized now that both had treated the other hands the same. I was no exception.

As I kicked my boots beneath the bunk and stood up to unbuckle my belt, I glanced toward the dimness where Slack's body was outlined in the bunk.

I froze, watching.

Slack had twisted on the thin mattress and was staring across the intervening space at Drake Martin's back. His right hand was running slowly up and down along the blanket, palm down, fingers spread wide.

I had seen the gesture before. Gunmen rubbing the sweat off their hands before making a draw!

Five

A message came up from Hilo the next day that a cattle barge Hollman had ordered from Honolulu would be in a week ahead of time. We had less than a day to round up the stock he wanted to cull from the herds and move them down to the coast for shipment to Oahu, where they would be butchered and the meat sold.

Ben Low was uttering guttural Chinese curses (or the equivalent, since the Chinese have no actual curse words) as he led the rest of us toward the valley where the culls were loosely gathered. The hands had been driving them in on Hollman's orders even before I arrived, but they had expected an added week for moving them to the tiny inlet for loading.

"I no be here next time dis hopp'n," Low promised. "Quit soon now and see New York, like I long time say."

I knew only what Hollman had told me and didn't learn until later that a prominent tourist had once seen him ride and had told him he should try America and the annual rodeo in Madison Square Garden. Since that, he had constantly talked of making the trip, even making tentative plans, but everyone on the ranch, from Hollman down, called it a dream. What chance did a *paniolo* have in the world rodeo championships against the nation's best?

I wondered, years later, what Hollman and the others

thought when the stubby Chinese rider did appear in the Garden and won the championship.

Hollman had told me of his plan to pattern the herd after what the Parkers already had started. He would introduce new Hereford and Brahma blood and attempt to develop a heavier meat animal. But first, he wanted to rid the ranch of the poorer breeding stock on hand. That was what we were after now—a bunch of aging cows or those that showed their poor beef stock.

It was barely daylight when we rode into the valley and Low, as foreman, called a halt. Below us, spread across the floor of the valley, we could make out the dark shapes of cows and calves. Even in the half-light I could distinguish the thin, bony shapes of some of the older animals and wondered whether there might be a streak of tuberculosis running through these animals that Hollman wanted to unload. Or maybe, as he said, it was just age. Once they were butchered, no one would know.

"Bunch 'em and push 'em downa valley," Low instructed in his stilted, high-pitched English. "Maybeso some good cows, you pick 'em out. Only poor go."

It was twenty miles to the beach and we had to have them there before sundown, he had been told by Hollman. We were going to lose what little meat was on them in that push, but at least the ranch would be rid of them.

In issuing instructions, Low ordered me to sweep along one flank with him, while Slack, one of the Hawaiian riders and Drake Martin were to move them in from the other side of the flat valley floor. More riders would be in the lead and riding drag on the drive, cutting out whatever good stock may have strayed into the herd.

Martin and Slack galloped off with the third rider, allowing the *paniolo* to ride between them. I had been watching them ever since Low awakened us in the black dampness of predawn to tell us of the change in plans. Neither Jeff nor the younger man had spoken, nor had they even looked at each other when they could avoid it. Now they seemed to spread out on each side of the *paniolo* in an unconscious effort to get as much distance between each other as possible.

Because of the urgency of the job, we had moved out without eating, but shortly before noon, as half the crew kept the cattle moving, the rest of us dismounted at a hurried encampment that Joe Tam had thrown up ahead of us, preparing a meal of rice and some of the fish we had caught at the *hukilau* the previous day. When we had finished, we rejoined the herd, pushing it as hard as we dared, while the other *paniolos* turned back to eat.

Low told me that the message concerning the barge had come up shortly after midnight and that Tam had immediately quit the fantan game, loaded his supplies in a wagon and taken off for the spot where we had caught up with him.

Shortly after noon, the valley narrowed to a high-walled gully which had been worn through the black lava. It was devoid of moving air, and the hooves of the horses and cattle left a thick haze of volcanic dust hanging over us, marking our progress. Soon it was impossible to tell Hawaiians from white men—*haoles*, as the Islanders called us—for our faces and clothing, wet with perspiration, were coated with the black grime.

Numerous branch trails and pockets led off the main trail, and all of us were hard put to keep the now thirsty and weary cattle from turning into them, leaving the main body. Curses and blasphemies in Hawaiian, Chinese, Portuguese and several other languages hung on the darkened air until we suddenly broke clear.

At this point, Ben Low called a halt and rode to the head of the drive, gathering the other riders about him.

The trail had led downward from the high valley, and now I could see the lagoon, which was our goal, several miles ahead, but between us lay a veritable jungle of thorns.

Keawa trees, Low called them. None were more than a dozen feet in height, but their nearly leafless, spine-lined branches were interlocked in a closely knit wall.

"This is hard part," Low said. Although he spoke to all of us, he seemed to be looking at Slack, Martin and myself. After all, the native *paniolos* had been through the experience many times before.

"If they get into the trees, it will take days to drive 'em out," Low said slowly, picking his English for our benefit. "We get torn up bad doin' it. Trail's wide, so we move 'em fast and straight down trail. Keep 'em goin' and no chance to get away from us."

I had worked brush country in South Texas as a kid, driving cattle out of swamps and bogs, but this was something different. I'd never heard of a cattle drive through a jungle. I didn't see how Low was going to do it.

But he accomplished it just as it was outlined. All of the riders were moved either ahead of or behind the cattle, with no flank riders. There wasn't room enough on the trail for them and the tightly bunched cattle, some stumbling with weariness.

Low and a trio of his Hawaiian riders led off, setting the pace, while the rest of us brought up the rear, whooping and shouting at the listless, thirsty animals, slashing at their backs with rope ends and quirts until they broke into a slow, hesitant trot. Those in the rear, horns tossing, low bellows coming from their lungs, crowded those ahead into the same uneven gait.

At several points, holes appeared in the rank walls of vegetation that flanked us on each side, and one of the riders with Low would drop into it, keeping curious animals from taking this divergent course. When the herd had passed, they fell in with us at the rear.

Once, an old cow and her half-grown calf sought to turn aside and push their way in among the keawa trees. Drake Martin, seeing what was happening, attempted to spur for-

ward along the flank of the drive, which filled the trail from
one wall of thorns to the other, and turn the wayward animals back to the herd.

Instead, the rider frightened the cow and calf as well as
several others, and all plunged into the jungle-like growth,
disappearing from sight. Martin, spurring his rearing horse
after them, also disappeared.

As the last of the herd passed the spot, the cattle crashed
through the thorny barrier and into the trail. When Drake
and his mount emerged several seconds later, his hat was
missing, and blood streaked the chest of the horse. The
rider's shirt was torn in several places, and there was a long
scratch across the same cheek that bore the ragged scar. He
held a handkerchief to his face, soaking up the blood flow,
and muttering curses that became edged with bitterness as
one of the Hawaiians attempted to joke with him.

Low's strategy was successful enough so that when we
finally emerged upon a flat, marshy area bordering the
lagoon, he estimated that no more than half a dozen head
had escaped into the brush. He was satisfied.

There was no sign of the barge onto which the animals
were to be loaded, nor was there any sign of a dock or loading ramp. There was nothing but a wide stretch of water-
packed sand ringing the lagoon.

The cattle picked up their pace as we broke onto the
open plain and the leaders veered to one side, while Low
and those riding point swung aside to let them pass. There
was a shallow depression holding a pool well back from the
beach. The thirst-crazed animals ran into it, horns tossing,
pushing aside their neighbors in their eagerness to slake
their thirst after the hot, dry drive.

I gathered that the fresh water drained into the natural
pond from the jungle above, although I couldn't figure what
kept the salt water from seeping in through the bottom
during high tide. Low explained that built-up coral formed
the bottom of the pool, keeping sea water out.

"Night's rest and water, maybeso they put back somea the meat we run off," Low offered sagely. "Next time Hollman wanta make da kine drive, he come hisself. I no be here."

"You mean there's some other way?"

He nodded. "She take maybe four day, but no lava, no thorns to get 'em here. This time no time for that."

I asked where the barge was, and received an answer that it would probably come around from Hilo during the night and be anchored in the lagoon before morning. Low explained that, even if the barge arrived during the afternoon, it would be impossible to get all of the cattle aboard before nightfall.

"No rifles yet. Hollman bring 'em by'mby," he explained simply.

Rifles? Then I remembered the carbine that hung on the wall of Mark's office. I had assumed it to be nothing more than a relic of his Texas days, but knowing his hatred for weapons and the violence that went with them, I should have realized he kept it for a more practical reason.

"Cows all swim out to barge," Low explained briefly. "We put *paniolos* in boats with rifles. They keep off sharks. Blood from maybe just one cow, all sharks go crazy. Sometimes cripple half the herd."

He was grinning at my ignorance, as a doctor of philosophy might upon the thoughts of an idiot, and I wondered whether he was remembering my crack about riders who tied themselves to horses and was putting me in my place.

"Anyone ever get hurt in this kind of loading?" I asked him, looking out across the smooth surface of the lagoon. I expected to see shark fins cutting the water. There was nothing but the reflection of the fast-sinking sun casting a trail of fire across the water.

The *paniolo* spread his hands in noncommittal fashion, offering a shrug as he stared at the water. Then he turned back to me with a serious, troubled scowl.

"What'sa mattah you *haoles?*" he asked, the pidgin which was universal among his riders becoming more pronounced. Normally he attempted to use his best English on me, Slack and Martin, reserving the dialect for the hands. He was gazing at me quizzically as I turned in my saddle to stare at him.

"What're you getting at?"

He shifted his gaze past me, and I looked to see Martin riding away from a group of riders, while Jeff Slack was just joining them. All were at the edge of the pool, away from the cattle, allowing their horses to drink from a corner which had not been turned to mud by the eager, horn-rattling herd.

"I think maybeso them two no like. Maybeso by'mby one big fight." He chuckled thoughtfully at the prospect, and I suddenly wondered whether he had really been in the bunkhouse the previous night during the fight at the corral, or whether he had taken note of the dust on Slack's clothing after the exchange.

I shrugged and shook my head, looking away.

"That's their trouble, not mine."

But he was right. During the entire drive they had stayed as far apart as possible without it interfering with the job. They hadn't spoken to each other even when brought together for instructions.

And I remembered Slack's strange movements—the mark of the gunslinger—when he stared at Drake's back, and the same feeling of well-being I had experienced then came back. If there was going to be trouble, it would flare between those two. I wouldn't be involved.

Under Ben's instructions, we bedded down the cattle, and some of the riders rode down to the beach, where they stripped off their clothing to frolic naked in the lagoon until Joe Tam arrived with his wagon and began putting together a quick meal.

One of the *paniolos* turned to and helped by building a fire and hanging an old black kettle over it, while the rest of us drew lots to see who would take the three night watches over the cattle.

Slack cursed roundly as he drew the first watch and glanced enviously at Martin, who had drawn a short stick and was among those of us excused. Two of the Hawaiians were to follow Jeff.

"Them damned cows are too old and tired to even move, let alone stampede," Jeff told Low in a tone that was heavy with sarcasm. "Night herd on them's a waste of talent."

Ben shook his head with Oriental blandness but an attitude that would not be swayed. "Rainy season, she come soon," he declared solemnly. "Better maybeso we watch 'em now and no have to chase 'em through keawe in dark."

As tin plates and cups were broken out from the back of the battered old wagon, Mark Hollman and Kimo rode in out of the dusk and a man hurried to unsaddle their horses and put them on picket ropes, as the rest of us had already done with our own mounts.

Hollman, I noticed, had ridden in with the carbine from his office thrust in a scabbard on his saddle, and carrying its mate balanced across the pommel. He put both of the weapons in the bed of the wagon before stepping into the chow line, with Kimo trailing behind him.

The fare was the same as at noon, but Tam had cut up the fish and boiled it and the rice into a thick chowder. Some hard crackers and coffee made up the rest of the meal.

Low and the others attacked the mixture with chopsticks, which they seemed to always carry with them, deftly picking out the pieces of fish and clotted bits of rice and popping them into their mouths, while they chattered continuously in half a dozen languages constantly punctuated by the always present pidgin terms.

Through either Hollman's thoughtfulness or his own, Kimo had brought metal spoons for Slack, Martin and me,

although he and Mark squatted at the edge of the fire, joining in the talk and scooping up their food with the awkward-
looking slivers of wood, finally tipping up the shallow plates
to gulp down the remaining broth. If the people back in
Texas could see Mark Hollman now, I reflected, they'd
never believe it.

As they finished eating, the men stood up and walked off
to the beach, singly and in pairs, to scour the tins with sand
and wash them with sea water. Joe Tam banked up the coals
beneath the black kettle and put a lid on it to leave the
chowder simmering. We would get it again for breakfast, I
knew. Surrounded though they were by beef day after day,
fish and rice still were the chief staples of the Hawaiian
riders.

I strolled through the darkness to the water's edge to
clean my own plate and the iron spoon. As I stooped in the
sand, pausing to watch the upper rim of the full moon push
slowly up out of the ocean beyond the quiet water, I heard
a sound behind me and glanced around. Slack was on his
haunches cleaning his own gear in the sand. He was paying
no attention to his work, but was staring at me instead.

"You takin' any sides in that business at the corral last
night, Turk?" His voice was low but harsh as he asked the
question.

"Just trying to stop trouble before it can start, like I told
you. I've known Mark Hollman a long time, and he won't
stand for it."

He glanced down at the tin plate in his hands, seeming to
accept my answer. He was wondering how much of the
conversation I had overheard between Drake and himself
before the start of the fight. And he was wondering whether
I might go to Hollman and tell what he had said about Malia.
He didn't want that, I could tell.

He looked up, his eyes flat and yellow in the thin moonlight. They slitted with thoughtfulness as he stared at me for
a long time before speaking.

"I know you from some place, Turk. Ever spend any time in Mexico?"

I shook my head as I stood up and banged the spoon against the pan to knock away the sand. "Never been there."

"I still know you from somewhere. I'll figure it out directly," he promised as I turned away, dipped my utensils into the edge of a small wave, then left him there, a dark, ugly disfigurement on the white face of the sand.

That was the first night in over twenty years that I had slept wrapped in a saddle blanket with a saddle beneath my head for a pillow, and I slept poorly at first, waking several times to see the dull glow of coals beneath Joe Tam's iron pot and to think of the lone man out there riding a slow circle around the bedded cattle.

Slack thought he knew me. But where? I had no idea. He was at least ten years younger than I, too young to have been on either side during the cattle war. If he had been behind those stone walls at Huntsville, I would have remembered him. They came and they went, but you remembered their faces. All of them. There was little else to do.

I awoke once more after the moon had gone down, as I thought I felt something moving near me. Dew had turned my blankets wet and, after lying tense for a moment without hearing anything more, I pulled them closer about me and soon went back to sleep.

Hollman himself awakened us before dawn and we saddled up, riding out to get the cattle on their feet and move them once more toward the water hole, while Tam punched up the fire beneath our skimpy breakfast. It was just growing light as we scoured out our plates once more and carried them back to the wagon, where the Chinese cook collected them.

Mark stood beside the rear wheel inspecting the two carbines. As I stopped beside him he glanced at me, then turned to hand one of the weapons to Kimo.

"Be careful, boy. It's loaded," he cautioned.

"Who's doing the shooting?" I asked, and Hollman looked up again sharply, staring into my eyes with a scowl.

"I'm hoping there won't be any sharks to worry about," he growled, "but if so, Kimo'll be on the one flank, Rodriques on the other. Best shots I've got."

I opened my mouth to remind him there was another, then snapped it shut. He didn't want me even to handle one of the rifles. We had already talked too much about me and guns. He wouldn't want the two of us in close company.

"I want to talk with you when we get back to the ranch, Sam," Mark said gruffly. "Ben and I had a talk last night, and there are some things I want to go over with you."

Before I could ask for any kind of explanation, Rodriques, a Portuguese rider with a broad grin and a drooping mustache, came up to take the other carbine, checking it as he walked away. Hollman turned to look out to the lagoon, and my eyes followed his.

I hadn't noticed it before nor had I heard the low drone of the powerful engine, but a heavy tugboat had moved a long, wooden-sided hulk into place and was now swinging back out of the way. Men ran about the deck of the barge, apparently anchoring her in position. Already two small boats had been launched from her, and oarsmen were pulling toward the shore. The light was still dim, and the seamen carried lanterns as they scurried about their work, but I was able to make out the shape of the bulky, ill-shaped vessel.

She lay low in the water, and I could see the timbers protruding above the railing that cut her into individual pens. Kimo had tried to explain the layout to me once, but I had not understood it until now. The separate enclosures allowed those aboard to load the cattle evenly, driving them into position and keeping the vessel on an even keel throughout the operation.

A wide ramp ran down into the water, and heavy wooden cleats were bolted to it. While I watched, one of the men started to put bags of sand over the wood to make it appear more stable for the animals and to keep them from slipping back into the water once they were started up.

"Why'n hell don't they come in closer than that?" I asked Hollman as he continued to stare past me at the preparations. "It's more'n two hundred yards out there."

"Coral reef. They could get in over it, but loaded, they'd never get out. They'd tear the bottom right out of that tub."

"You mean we're going to swim them critters clear out there and try to run them up that ramp."

He looked at me with a knowing grin as he said, with a touch of sarcasm, "They was doin' it for twenty years b'fore I got here. Best way we've figured yet. Besides," he explained, "when them cows see that ramp, they get real eager to get onto something dry. For big shipments, we bring in the big cattle boat from Honolulu and hoist them aboard with slings."

The *paniolos* were pulling off their heavy boots and throwing them into the back of the wagon before swinging once more into their saddles. Several stripped off the rest of their clothing as well, mounting in the nude. It was a strange procession that started toward the water hole.

I removed my boots and swung into the saddle, following, and noticing that both Drake Martin and Jeff Slack had left their boots behind, taking a lesson from the more experienced Islanders.

As I glanced over my shoulder, Hollman also was removing his boots and was swinging up onto his mount, while Kimo and Rodriques were sauntering toward the two boats that were being pulled up onto the sand by the seamen. Each had one of the carbines slung loosely in the crook of his arm.

With Ben Low in the lead, the men circled the cattle, some urging their mounts into the coral-bottomed pool to drive the sullen, still tired animals from where they stood belly-deep in the clouded water. Rope ends and quirts, along with a good deal of swearing, were used to drive them toward the edge of the lagoon.

Actually, the formation of riders formed a tight V-shaped outline, hemming in the bawling cows and the skittish, nervous calves, forcing them across the strip of tide-packed sand. As the first animals hit the salt water, they halted, standing up to their hocks in foam, shivering with fright. The riders pressed forward, swinging braided ropes across their backs or reaching down to grab their tails, twisting until the cows, lowing in pain, plunged deeper, the calves following in desperate, floundering fashion.

With Kimo in one boat, the Portuguese marksman in the other, the men from the barge had pushed off the beach, one on each flank of the thoroughly frightened herd.

I was in the middle of the line of riders forming the "V" on the lefthand side. Ahead of me, the boat bearing Kimo and the carbine formed the lead element, acting as a corner of a floating gate, so to speak, through which the cattle were directed. The boat, maneuvered by the oarsman's practiced strokes, continued to pull slowly ahead, literally aiming the leaders of the herd toward the ramp extending downward below the surface from the barge.

As my horse, a heavy-bodied animal with guts and stamina, moved forward, snorting his nervousness, the warm water crept up over my bare ankles, then soaked through the legs of my trousers. Just as the animal started to swim, stepping off a coral ledge and sinking until only his head and neck were above water, a cow swung toward me, threshing water in an effort to turn back to land. With water striking me just under the armpits, I was able to swing the end of my lariat across her nose with a wet crack that turned her back to the others.

Suddenly a rider ahead of me shouted something, and I looked up to see Kimo rise in the bow of the boat and aim at the water to the left. A lone fin was cutting the surface past the prow of the vessel.

The weapon bucked in his hands as the explosion echoed over the backs of the milling cattle. There was a sharp flurry on the water, and the fin disappeared.

There was a shout to my rear, and I glanced back to where Slack was waving, indicating something in front of me. The same cow I had turned back before had taken advantage of my laxity and was swimming away from the herd, cutting between myself and the Hawaiian rider ahead of me.

I gave the horse his head and he swung out to cut off the wild-eyed cow and the laboring calf that followed her. Frantically she threshed the water in an attempt to outdistance the horse, but finally turned back, almost drowning the calf as she lurched clumsily against it.

The horse turned to follow her, kicking water with powerful strokes that brought spray boiling up into my face. The salt burned my eyes, blinding me. As I fought to wipe my face with the sleeve of my free arm, I heard the rifle crack again. I caught a glimpse of an object churning in the surf only a few yards away, and the foam turned suddenly red.

Glancing toward the wayward cow, I saw that she had not given up, but had swung about on the edge of the herd and was trying to move away, the calf still struggling at her side. As I bent in the saddle to reach for her tail and swing her abruptly about, I felt something snap below the surface. Suddenly, my feet still entangled in the stirrups, I was thrown clear of my mount and over the back of the frightened cow.

I heard a shout of alarm just before I slid down between several of the threshing animals. Water pushing through my nose and into my sinuses, I was still fighting to get clear of the saddle. I felt my bare feet slip from the stirrups and began flailing my arms wildly to regain the surface. Salt and sand burned my eyes, and I choked on a mouthful of water as I floundered in the midst of a melee of kicking hooves and hairy bodies. A sharp hoof caught the front of my shirt and I felt the sodden tearing of fabric.

Then I was fighting, clawing my way up between two of the animals until my head was above water. I caught one swift glimpse of some of the cows already being prodded up the ramp and onto the barge, the two boats now hemming them in on each flank. There was an excited shout behind me then. It was Slack's voice.

"Keep them movin' or they'll all be shark bait!" he cried.

Remembering the blue fins, fear seemed to paralyze my lungs, and I fought for air as two of the fear-wild cows pressed against me, back and chest, grinding their bony frames against me in their own efforts to keep afloat. Suddenly one of them lunged forward, and I was thrown, choking on sea water, back beneath the surface.

But with new breath in my lungs, I slipped from between the pressing bodies and swam for the bottom, angling toward where I thought the edge of the herd should be. Once I half turned on my back and saw that the swirl of hooves, sand and bodies was behind me. The walls of my chest seemed near the point of exploding as I fought my way to the surface and floundered helplessly, my strength running out of my fingertips like water through a rain spout.

"Turk! Catch it!"

As I turned in the water, a noose slapped the surface beside me. Weakly I snatched at it, managing to get one arm through the loop before it tightened. Mark Hollman was at the other end, taking turns about the saddle horn as he drove his nearly submerged mount toward shore. He slid from the saddle, hand-gripping the animal's mane as he sought to lighten the load. The animal slowed as it struck the coral shelf, then lunged forward with solid footing, nearly jerking my arm from its socket. My curse was drowned in the swell that swept over me.

Hollman, leading the animal, dragged me up onto the sand, then slackened the rope, dropping it as he turned to run toward me. I sat up slowly, then hunched over on hands and knees as my breakfast, mixed with salt water, soaked into the sand. Mark's hand gripped my shoulder as I slowly raised my head, looking at him through wet eyes.

"You okay, Sam?" His voice was anxious.

"I'll make it."

"You just stay here and rest. Don't even move till we get this job done," he ordered gruffly. I heard his bare feet crunch on the sand as he returned to his horse and watched as he rode past me to plunge the animal into the surf and swim toward the barge.

The *paniolos,* some of them swimming their horses behind reluctant cattle, bending to twist the tails of the animals and force them up the ramp or to help the tired, frightened calves find a foothold on the rough timbers, were a tight circle about the barge. Most of the cattle had been forced up the ramp and directed into pens.

I dropped back on the sand and closed my eyes. Vaguely I heard the shouts of success from across the water as the chore was completed and, a few minutes later, a grating sound on the sand near me. A moment later, something dropped beside me with a sodden thud, and I opened my eyes to find Kimo staring down at me with serious intent.

"I dive for your saddle, Mister Turk. Maybe somebody think you not swim so good."

I pushed myself up, and the sickness started to well up from my stomach, the taste of salt still thick on my tongue.

"The cinch," he said slowly. "I think she was cut!"

I stared at him for an instant, sickness forgotten, fear replacing it. I rolled to my knees and grabbed the leather cinch strap, staring at the neat slice that went most of the way through. Fear gripped me. I hadn't run far enough . . .

Six

"Ben means it this time," Hollman told me. "He's drawn his pay and is taking a boat for the States. He's packing his stuff now. That means I need a ramrod."

I just nodded, waiting for him to go on. I hadn't told him about the cut cinch strap, and I had passed it off to Kimo by telling him my fall into the milling herd had resulted from my own carelessness. He was dubious of my explanation that the strap had been partially cut years before when I had ridden into a barbed-wire fence in the dark, but he had said nothing to anyone about it, I was sure.

"Think you can handle the job?" Hollman asked bluntly.

I shook my head, allowing the horse to drop his hoof and hanging the clippers on the corral rail.

"I don't know, Mark. I think I can, but I don't know what these *paniolos* might think of me. I had a little disagreement with one or two of them a while back."

"I know about that. I asked Ben what he thought, and he figures you're the man for the job. Said you straightened yourself out with the boys the other night, when you admitted they knew more about fantan than you did."

"That's all it took?" I was a little surprised. "You seem to know more about what's going on around here than I figured."

"I try to know without fostering any tale-tellers," the ranch manager admitted. "When I want to know something, I ask a straight question and expect that kind of an answer. The boys know that and respect it. I'll expect the same of you, but you'll be allowed a free hand in running the outfit. All I want to be sure of is that you're working for me and that I have your loyalty. That's important."

"If you've got any questions on that score, maybe you'd do better to find yourself another man to start," I told him. His distrust when I had first arrived, the fear he had expressed that the old flame of violence was still smoldering somewhere inside me, wasn't hard to recall.

"I ain't got any question on it, Sam. You know I've been watching you. Maybe even riding you some," he admitted. "I just wanted to hear you say it."

"Why not one of the boys that's been with you a while? One of the Hawaiians? Don't you reckon one of them'd maybe make a better foreman than me?"

"They know their work and they do it when there's someone to tell them," he said, "but most of them are too happy-go-lucky to hold down this kind of chore. With these Island people, life was made for having fun. Cattle ranching here, like anywhere else, don't come in that category."

"Okay, Mark. I'm your man, but I want it understood *I'm* the foreman. I expect my decisions to be backed up."

He stuck his hand out, nodding, with a grin. "You're the boss man. The job pays eighty bucks a month, and I promise you'll earn it."

I didn't have to be told that. More than once I had seen Ben Low have to break up a fight, when a pair of the *pani-olos* didn't see things the same way. I wasn't nearly as sure as Mark Hollman that I was the man he wanted. I recalled the attitude of the Chinese cook, Tam, following my earlier criticism of Ben Low's habit of tying himself on a horse's back, and wondered how having me as ramrod would set with him and some of the other old hands.

"Come up to the office tonight, and I'll give you a run-down on some of the things I have in mind in the future for the place," Hollman said, as he turned and sauntered stoop-shouldered toward the house.

I turned to pick the heavy hoof nippers off the fence as Ben Low came out of the bunkhouse and raised a hand to attract my attention.

"You the new boss, huh!" he declared, grinning at me with pleasure.

"In name, at least. I don't know whether I'll be able to handle that horde of yours or not."

He leaned against the rail, his black, slanted eyes surveying me thoughtfully, the smile still on his lips as he nodded.

"No *pilikia* with them, Turk. I pass the word last night that I want you to take my place. They like you. No trouble."

"Thanks, Ben. You didn't have to do that, but I appreciate the backing. It'll make the job a lot easier if we all get along."

"Maybeso I see you no more," he declared, the smile fading. "Speak *aloha* now."

He extended his hand through the rails, and I took it.

"Leaving so soon? You made up your mind in a big hurry."

He shook his head, the grin coming back. "Mind made up a long time. Just didn't decide till the other day, when you nearly drowned with them cows.

"That same thing could happen to any of us whenever we make that kind of drive," he went on slowly. "Maybeso I want to see some more of the world before it happen to me."

"Just an accident. My own fault for not checking the rigging first."

He was still grinning, except for his eyes. They were staring into mine. "Kimo, he tell me about cut. I look. Take long barb to cut through alla way like that."

Then I hadn't fooled Kimo as I had thought, I realized. I wondered whether he had mentioned it to anyone besides Ben Low. The Chinese read my thoughts and shook his head.

"Don't worry, Turk. Kimo tell no one else. He promise me."

"Promise you? Why that?"

He shook his head, his attitude again thoughtful. "I think so if you want to tell about it to anyone, you would. You don't speak, so why should I? Why should Kimo?"

"It didn't seem that important, Ben. In fact, I'd forgotten about it till you just brought it out now."

"I betcha." His tone was cynical with disbelief. "I tell you one thing, Turk. No Island boy do a thing like that. They know I kick hell from them, they do. Who do you think that leave?"

The smile on my own face felt like a death mask drying across the skin as I forced a shrug. "That does kind of narrow the field, don't it?"

Kimo drew up before the door of the bunkhouse in a spring wagon, looking toward us and shouting, "Ben-san, whatsa mattah you? Pretty soon now, she get dark!"

"Kimo's taking me down to Hilo," Low explained. "I catcha boat tomorrow. Get other boat in Honolulu."

"I know some folks back in Texas, where you might get a job if you run out of money."

He shook his head, the grin growing more broad. "No run out of money. Long time now I save. Have no place to spend. I not run out."

I shook his hand again and went back to trimming the horse's hooves as he shouted Chinese obscenities at Kimo's urgings for him to hurry. He shouted to me once more and waved as he rolled away past the ranch house, his saddle and belongings in the rear of the wagon. I waved back, frowning. The thoughts he had left me with were not pleasant.

I had done a lot of thinking about that slashed cinch strap and I had recalled my awaking the night before the loading of the stock on the offshore barge was to take place. I had thought I heard someone moving about but had dismissed it and gone back to sleep. Whoever had attempted to make shark bait of me had probably cut the leather there in the dark while I slept.

Low apparently had failed to mention what he had learned to Mark Hollman, or the ranch manager certainly would have questioned me about it before this, I realized, but Low's assurance that none of the Hawaiians had done it bothered me.

In mulling it over, I had half convinced myself that Tam or one of the *paniolos* might have slashed the cinch strap as a practical joke, not realizing how deadly it could be. After I had nearly drowned among the churning bodies of the cattle there in the lagoon, the culprit would have been afraid to laugh at it, let alone confess, I decided.

But Ben Low had practically put his finger—three fingers, in fact—on the possible suspects. The newcomers: Drake Martin, Jeff Slack, or even Himmler, the sad-eyed book-keeper. The latter could have cut the leather before we had even left the ranch, although I doubted it. The strain on the hide during the rough drive through the lava wastes and the keawe jungle almost certainly would have caused it to part before we reached the beach.

I had accepted the job of foreman mostly for the money and because Mark had laid it on the line that he thought I was the man for the job. I owed him whatever he asked of me, and taking over for Ben Low had been only small payment.

Now, though, as I worked over the last of the horse's hooves, cutting away the heavy cartilage, then smoothing off the edges with a wood rasp to keep the hoof from splitting, I realized I had done myself a favor. As foreman, I would have a chance to watch the three men who had arrived at the ranch in my wake, to study them and attempt to learn which of them it was who wanted me dead!

During the months that had passed, that feeling of impending danger that had haunted me for so long had slowly slipped away. Even when the saddle strap had been cut, I had attempted to minimize it, dismissing it as a prank, but now the feeling of fear was back, reclaiming my nerves. My hands were shaking on the rasp as I finished the hoof and allowed the horse to drop it.

I was about to slip the halter off and turn the animal loose among the others in the corral, when the pounding of hooves attracted my attention. I looked to the other side of the enclosure to see Malia approaching at a fast gallop. Her hair, usually swept beneath her hat, was flying loose and long as she sat straight in the saddle. Behind her, approaching at an angle, was Jeff Slack, spurring his mount as though to overtake her.

I unbuckled the halter, and the horse snorted his surprise at sudden freedom as he whirled and trotted to join the others which were gathered on the opposite side of the corral near the bars. I untied the halter and started across the corral as Malia dismounted and Slack drew up beside her, swinging down.

"I'll unsaddle him for you," he told the girl as he reached out to take the bridle of her mount. She looked at him as though surprised at this show of gallantry, then nodded acceptance.

"Thank you. I did not see you coming," she said, starting to turn away.

"I reckon if it'd been young Martin you'd of seen him." The smile that had been on Slack's face was gone, and his expression matched the surliness in his tone. The girl turned to look at him with a frown. Not knowing why, I halted, still unseen by either, the horses now shielding me from view.

"What do you mean?" the girl asked sharply.

"Don't worry. I ain't going to tell your old man how you and the kid are always sneaking off for them long rides of yours, but it'd be a lot easier for me to hold my tongue if you'd treat me as nice as you do him just once in a while."

Slack's voice was low and sounded like a bucket of gravel

as he mouthed the words, each syllable heavy with suggestion. Malia stood staring at him for a moment, her breasts
rising and falling rapidly as her anger mounted.

"A girl as pretty as you ought to pass her charms around
a little. There's just too much of you for one man to handle,"
Slack told her, grinning.

The words were hardly out of his mouth when she leaped
toward him, striking him heavily across the cheek with her
gloved hand. The smile was still on his lips, but it was the
smile of a wolf with a cornered fawn as he grabbed her
wrist, speaking between his teeth harshly, as he twisted her
arm.

"Now, you wouldn't want Mister Hollman to hear all
about this, would you, ma'am? And you don't really reckon
I think you're all as royal as you try to put on. You're a
woman, and I don't reckon they change much in any part of
the world." The words were said softly, almost soothingly,
as he continued to grin at her, seemingly unaware of the
pain that twisted her face, caused by his grip on her wrist.

She said something to him in Polynesian, her voice a low
hiss, and he laughed.

"Now that ain't no way to talk to a feller that's just trying
to protect your interests and keep you and young Martin
from getting into trouble with your old man."

"He'll kill you when I tell him about this!" she snarled at
him.

Slack shook his head, enjoying himself. "You ain't going
to tell him. You know it. I know it. So let's quit playing them
kind of games." He twisted her arm more, and the girl
gasped in pain. "You're going to be nice to me. Real nice,
ain't you."

"Let her be, Slack!"

The girl's eyes swung toward me in a show of surprise and
hope. For a moment, Slack didn't seem to hear me. Then
he released his hold and swung slowly to look at me out of
flat, yellow eyes. For an instant his wolfish grin seemed to

slip, then came back with equal broadness as the girl backed against the corral bars, looking from one of us to the other fearfully, breathing, choking past her lips, hair tumbling over her face.

"Well," Slack said chidingly, "if it ain't the quiet Texan!"

"You're through, Slack. Go pack your gear before the hands string you up from the nearest tree."

He stood staring at me, the lips still drawn back from his teeth, but his eyes were shrewd in judgment.

"You wouldn't tell no one about this little talk the girl and I was having," he decided.

"Maybe you'd like to repeat that with a rope around your neck!"

He relaxed, trying to look friendly and ashamed, allowing the corners of his mouth to droop.

"Now wait a minute, Sam. Maybe I got kind of carried away. I ain't afraid to say I'm sorry for what just happened." He turned his eyes on the girl as I started to slide between the corral bars. "You understand, don't you, Miss Malia? I didn't really mean nothing by what I said."

"Pack up," I repeated. "You've chased your last cow and your last woman here."

I was just straightening on his side of the fence when he came at me, lashing out with a pointed toe, aiming for my face. I twisted just enough to catch it on the shoulder and be slammed back against the corral bars. Slack came at me, all pretext gone, his yellow teeth bared in hatred, slamming a bone-hard fist against my teeth. Somewhere nearby, Malia moaned in terror, as I felt pain slash upward into my brain.

Another fist caught me just below the wishbone, and stars seemed to skyrocket out of my stomach, exploding in my head. Slack's breath was coming in harsh rushes, but somewhere behind the sound was a chuckle of glee. He enjoyed his work.

Whirling away, trying to avoid another body punch, I struck straight out at him, barely realizing I still held the heavy steel rasp, but feeling it as the blunt end of the tool pulled the wind out of his belly, driving deep.

He staggered backward, trying to keep his balance as my own head cleared and I moved in on him, the rasp held low and ready. He started to dodge, and I swung toward him. Suddenly his boot lashed out, catching me in the wrist, numbing it as the weapon went flying.

Slack dived for the rasp, but my own boot caught him in the side while he was still in mid-air, sending him rolling away to strike the ground heavily on his back. As I closed on him, his face was twisted with panic, saliva coming in a foamy stream from the corner of his mouth. He tried to scream but strangled on the sound, as I grabbed him by the shirt front and half raised him before slamming a fist full into his face.

His form went limp in my hand and I let him drop. His eyeballs rolled back, then the lids closed over them as he gasped heavily. Small puffs of dust rose around him, then settled, some of it mixing with the blood that flowed from his nose and broken lips.

I staggered backward to lean against the corral fence, panting heavily, my head whirling.

"How bad did you hurt him?" Malia asked, staring down at the still figure. "Is he dead?"

I looked away from her. "Get some water and throw it on him. He'll live to get off this range." My voice sounded harsh and strange in my own ears.

The girl hesitated, glancing at me, then at Slack.

"Do what I tell you!" I ordered. "Wet him down!"

She moved to the water trough built into the side of the corral and took down the pail that hung from one of the uprights. She dipped it in the water and carried it hesitantly toward the figure in the dust, glancing at me doubtfully. Still leaning against the fence for support, I nodded, and she tipped the bucket until water streamed across Slack's head and shoulders.

She stepped back quickly as he stirred, emitting a groan, then opened his eyes, staring up blankly for the moment that it took realization to sink in. Slowly, he sat up, staring at me as hatred darkened his eyes.

"You're pretty good in that kind of a fight, Turk," he said thickly. "Wonder how you'd be with a gun."

"You won't have a chance to find out. Get on your horse and get out of here," I told him, straightening and moving over to where the rasp had fallen. I picked up the heavy length of metal and balanced it in my hand as he started to rise.

"You talk like that's an order," he said slowly, trying to force the grin back on his face. His cut lips must have hurt too much. He gave up the effort and allowed hatred to be hatred without the trimmings.

"It's an order. I was made foreman less than an hour ago."

"Your first official act, huh?" He tried the grin again and almost made it. "Reckon you'd be a hard man to work for anyhow. What about my pay? I got some on the books."

"How much?"

"Sixty dollars."

"Leave the horse at the stable in Hilo, and I'll send down your money and your gear when I send someone after the mount."

He took a step forward, his face falling into a scowl. "Ain't you kind of rushing things, Turk?"

I hefted the rasp for effect. "Get up and ride, Slack. Try taking me again, and something might happen to that gun hand of yours!"

His eyes went to the tool for an instant, and his shoulders drooped as he turned slowly to his horse, pulling himself painfully into the saddle. He started to rein away, then halted, staring over his shoulder at me. The grin was back on his face, and his voice was so soft I could hardly hear it.

"I told you I knew about you, Turk," he said with a strange

thoughtfulness. "You'll be seeing me again, I reckon, but it'll be different than it was in that Texas street."

I gasped involuntarily, hearing the sound as air expanded my lungs.

"Yeah," he went on slowly, "only I won't be a poor old grocer for you to shoot at or a kid to chop up with a gun! I'll have a gun of my own!" He was still grinning as he turned in the saddle and spurred the horse to a trot, not looking back as he rode away.

"Sam?" The girl's voice was soft, almost as though afraid to speak to me. "Is he right? Did you kill someone?"

"I killed someone. A long time ago. Before you were born." I didn't look around as I heard her walking away toward the house.

Slack had known about it all the time, but if he was the one who had tried to kill me, who had followed me here, why? What reason would he have? It had happened so long ago. Thoughts were crawling over each other—thoughts tainted with fear—as I turned to Malia's horse and began to strip off the saddle.

Seven

The late-summer months turned into winter almost before I realized it, and I would not have known at all had it not been for the calendar leaves, the fact that the rains came, and that on clear mornings, Mauna Kea, the highest of the volcanic peaks, wore a coating of snow that ringed her crest.

I had ceased to worry over the fact that I had betrayed Mark Hollman's confidence in me less than an hour after he had made me his foreman. He had said that he wanted to know what went on about the ranch, but when he had called me into his office to ask my reason for firing Jeff Slack, I had simply told him that the rider had disobeyed an order, refusing to take my new appointment seriously.

Hollman had accepted the explanation and had impressed me again with the fact that I had his full backing in any such actions that I might want to take. As I left the office, however, I found Malia lurking near the door. She seemed confused at being discovered, and I realized that she had been listening to find out whether I had told the real reason for the gunman's dismissal. She said nothing as I passed her in the hallway, but her smile was enough to tell me she was thankful that I had neglected to bring out the true facts, which might drag Drake Martin into the discussion, as well as the secret meetings which Slack had mentioned.

I had continued to live in the bunkhouse with the rest of the men and had moved to the rear of the room, taking the bunk left vacant by Slack. Several times I had tried to draw young Martin into conversations concerning Malia and his plans for the future, but he guarded that connection with a jealousy that was only lightly cloaked by his attempt at innocent unconcern over the girl.

He did as he was told, showing all the marks of an experienced cowman, but most of the time he stayed apart from the others, lying in his bunk and reading at night by the dim light instead of taking part in the fantan games that had become a nightly affair. Tam, the cook, openly invited me to participate one night, and I lost more than a month's pay before I admitted, in my best sheepish manner, that I figured it took a Chinaman to beat a Chinaman at his own game.

The hands were working on a stone jug of *okolehao*, a native whiskey brewed from *ti* roots, and were pretty outspoken in their happiness over taking the ramrod to the cleaners and making him admit for the second time that this was not his game. Losing the money was worth it, though, for it seemed to loosen any tension that might still have existed between us. Before we went to bed, I stepped out to look at the sky for signs of rain, and found that Tam had followed me out. Standing there, weaving drunkenly on his feet, he had chuckled and slapped me on the back with one of his huge fire-calloused hands.

"Turk-san, you one pretty damn good *haole*," he declared. "Nex' time you get pay, we play fantan again maybeso by'mby."

"Not on your tintype," I growled at him. "That ain't no game for a *haole* to try against you *pake* bastards!"

He laughed aloud, seemingly pleased with my use of the Polynesian words. "*Haole*," I had learned early, was Hawaiian for "white man," while "*pake*" was used to designate the Chinese race.

Things were pretty routine until the first big rain, which had thunder and lightning to help it along. It resulted in one of the herds going through a fence and getting mixed up with the Parker herd. It took hands from both ranches more than a week to get them sorted out and back in the right pastures. After that, it took nearly another week to repair the fences that had been torn down. In making my report to Hollman, I found that he blamed the thunder and lightning for the stampede.

"It can rain pitchforks," he declared, "but it's damned seldom we get any of the noise to go with it. Don't reckon I've seen more than a dozen of them kind of storms since I've been here. Something new to them cows, too, I reckon."

He changed the subject before I had a chance to agree, asking from behind the coal-oil lantern on his desk, "How's young Martin working out? He pulling his weight?"

"He's doing fine. Don't have any complaints with him at all. You have any reason for asking?"

Himmler, who had been sitting at the other desk silently writing in a ledger, glanced up at this turn in the conversation, but went quickly back to his work as he saw me watching him.

"No." Hollman shook his head, frowning. "Just wondered how he was making out with the local boys. He never seems to have much to say."

"Sometimes that can save a man a heap of trouble," I offered, and Hollman looked up at me with the trace of a sardonic smile.

"I'll have to go along with your word on anything having to do with trouble, Sam," he said in slow agreement. "You know more about that commodity than anyone I know."

I was wondering about that last statement as I left and went across the yard and past the corner of the corral toward the bunkhouse. Maybe Hollman had figured there was more to the sudden departure of Jeff Slack than I had told him, or maybe he was just recalling some of the distant past that he had said he was willing to forget. And I wondered if Malia had brought that past back to life in his mind by trying to find out more about what had happened back in Texas, after what she had heard from Slack before he had ridden out.

Unless Hollman had business in Hilo, it usually was Kimo who was sent down to the coast twice a week for the mail, and I had made a point of asking him casually several times whether he had seen any sign of Slack. The boy had seen him twice, once standing in front of a seaman's hangout called "The Golden Dragon," and another time as he was walking along the street with a girl.

I had asked Kimo about the woman, but he was content to sniff with derision and comment in Polynesian on her morals, adding, for my benefit, that she was an entertainer at the bar where he had first seen the gunman.

But I felt that it was none of these things that was really bothering Hollman, though. The real reason had come out in his question about Drake Martin. He was worried—even jealous, perhaps—of the attention Malia was showing the young cowman.

I had seen the first signs of it that day on the beach, when she was attempting to teach him to play the ukulele, teasing him and laughing at his efforts. Hollman had attempted to ignore the incident, but even as he was talking to me, his disturbance had shown through. Later, he and I had ridden out to look over one of the herds and he had spotted the rider and the girl sitting close together on a hillside, talking, while Martin's horse grazed a dozen yards away.

"You might tell that kid that I'm paying him as a rider, not as a lover," Hollman had growled at me.

I mentioned the matter the next evening, when I found Martin turning his horse into the corral, and he stood eying me coldly.

"If there was anything going on that he doesn't like, we wouldn't have been sitting out in the open like that," he told me. "I'll tell him myself, if you want."

"I'm just passing on his feelings about what he's paying

you to do," I replied. "And I'm with him on that. You're paid to ride."

There had been no more such incidents during the day, but several times in the evening I had seen Drake saddle two horses, riding one away, while he left the other tied in the corral. Once, I was standing in the doorway of the bunkhouse, when Malia slipped through the darkness to lower the bars and ride the second animal out into the night in the same direction taken by Martin.

, I wondered if this was the type of thing that Hollman expected me to report to him, and made a point of ignoring it. Where Drake Martin rode after working hours was no concern of mine, and Malia was Hollman's daughter. If he couldn't control her, it was no affair of mine. She didn't come under the same heading as horses and cattle, and they were what I had been hired to handle.

Having spent some time alone with Hollman in his office, listening to tales of the past and plans for the future, through which was woven the story of the years since he had left Texas, it wasn't hard to understand his feeling.

Often he would sit for minutes at a time, even during a business discussion, looking up at the painting of his long-dead wife, and whenever Malia came into the room, he would maneuver her close to the painting so that the likeness of the mother and daughter could be compared.

"Someday you'll be as pretty as your mother," he told her more than once. Then he would turn back to his work, while she slipped quietly from the office.

When Mark Hollman lost his Hawaiian wife, he had lost the only thing that had really meant anything to him in his life. Back in Texas, his property, his self-respect had meant so little that he walked out on them when trouble threatened to erupt.

Later, when his wife died, he may have blamed himself for that in some unfathomable way, feeling that he was unable to aid her.

Judging from the girl's quiet, submissive manner whenever she was in the company of her father, he may have blamed her in early life for his wife's death, ignoring her to the point that she realized he held that death against her.

But as the girl matured, Mark obviously transferred to her the protection he had been unable to give his wife as she lay dying. As a result, the parental cloak was about her so tightly that she could smother beneath it without Hollman realizing what was happening. There was little doubt that Hollman's attempts to overcome his own feelings of guilt by making up for past failings were affecting the girl. Sooner or later, it would also affect Drake Martin. I couldn't help wondering what would happen then. Still, it was none of my damned business!

Then the nocturnal rides of Martin and the girl stopped abruptly. Sometimes, when the moon was up, the young man would saddle a horse and ride off from the ranch, returning late, after the lights were out in the bunkhouse, and several times I smelled native liquor on his breath the following morning, but usually he turned in early and lay with his face to the wall, seeming to ignore the good-natured noises from the other riders.

"Whassa mattah that boy?" Tam wanted to know one morning as I came up from the corral for a cup of coffee. "All time someone try to be friendly, an' he no speak."

"I don't know," I had to admit. "He's got troubles of his own, I reckon."

"Better so he forget the girl," Tam advised. "Mistah Hollman fire the last man take her for ride at night. Jus' one time an' *pau!*" He made a slashing gesture with his hand. "The one-time feller no have job."

The missionaries had brought Christmas to Hawaii, and while most of the Islanders still appeared to be a little dubious as to just what it meant, Mark Hollman announced there would be the annual three-day *luau.*

"That's a day to get ready, a day for the brawl, and a day to recover," he explained to me with a grin. "Besides, this kind of wraps up all of my Christmas gifts to the hands and their families in one package."

Meantime, Mark had ordered one of the hands to bring down from the hills a long-needled evergreen, which turned out to be a variety of fir, and this was set up in his office. Malia did the decorating, hanging it with tinsel, with glass balls which had been brought in years before from San Francisco, and with a white angel on top.

The day before Christmas, Mark summoned me to the office, and he and Malia presented me with a new shirt, which also had been ordered from the mainland. Neither was happy until I tried it on.

"You shouldn't have done anything like this," I told them. "I haven't had a chance to get anything for either of you."

"I know, but we ain't worried about it," Mark declared jovially. "You ain't been off this ranch since you got here, so how'd you ever of had a chance to get anything?"

That night in the bunkhouse, I noticed that Drake Martin also had a new shirt similar to the ones presented to Himmler and myself, but I doubted that Mark Hollman knew about it. It also explained the new woven horsehair bridle that I had seen hanging from the horn of Malia's saddle that afternoon. Drake probably had spent his spare time over the weeks weaving it, but I never had seen him working on it around the main ranch, nor had I noticed him collecting horsehair for its manufacture.

Hollman had been fretting that it would rain and spoil the *luau*, but Christmas Day dawned clear and bright with just a touch of frost in the air at the high altitude. Long before noon it had warmed up, and the families of the married employees were drifting in from the far corners of the ranch as they had for the earlier *hukilau*.

A wagon had been sent down to Hilo the previous day for extra provisions, and the women set about in a palm grove in a hollow behind the corral preparing the food, while some of the men began scooping out a huge hole in the ground and heating large rocks in several fires surrounding it. Others slaughtered and cleaned the several hogs which had been fattening since midsummer.

I watched as the hogs were lowered into the hole, carefully wrapped in banana leaves, layers of hot stones distributed for even heat, then covered over with dirt. Short, chunky Island bananas, also cloaked in leaves, were put in the hole to be baked by the heated rocks.

There was a festive spirit, and the air was filled with laughter as jugs of the locally brewed *okolehao* made the rounds among the men. Mark joined the men in their jokes and made a point of drinking as much as the rest. I pretended to suck on the jug, too, when it came my way, although I was careful of how much of the fire-flavored brew I actually allowed to flow down my throat.

"The mark of who is top man is in how much you can drink at a *luau*," Hollman had warned me earlier. "You're the foreman, and that means you've got to still be on your feet when the rest of them can't find their ass with both hands."

Drake Martin also was present and drank along with the rest, grinning at some of the jokes that were made, and at the glances that were cast toward some of the younger women as more and more of the jugs were emptied, but saying little.

Occasionally he would glance toward where Malia was working with the other women preparing food, then quickly look in another direction. Despite the exchange of Christmas gifts, I couldn't help but feel that something had gone wrong between the pair.

Malia was dressed in a tight-fitting sarong that ended just below her knees after being wrapped tightly across her breasts and about the waist. Some of the other, younger wives and the daughters of the hands wore similar garments, but the older women wore the sack-shaped Mother Hubbards.

"Them missionaries sure did their worst, when they dreamed up that cotton-print abortion," declared Hollman, swinging an arm to indicate one of the gowns. "Kind of a cross between a nightshirt and a flour sack. If they was trying to desex the women like they said, they couldn't have done no better with a scalpel." With a fair amount of the native whiskey warming his belly, he grew expansive and philosophical.

"Ever tell you what the natives say about the missionaries?" he asked, clapping me on the back as he passed the jug, again. "Say they came here to do good and did well. Damned missionary families own half the Islands. Dirty shame, too. No chance for the rest of us. No chance for the natives much, either." He laughed at the story. It seemed to be one of his favorites.

The *kalua* pig, as it was called, was unearthed late in the afternoon and was served on large sections of palm and banana leaf, along with the roast bananas, a kind of salad called *lomi lomi*, which I later found was raw salmon chopped fine and mixed with salt. There were rice balls, delicately prepared seaweed, bits of baked and fried octopus and squid, and other things I failed to recognize.

The men, joined now by the women, continued to drink the native liquor, and some were showing the effects as some of the younger girls began to dance in the center of the palm grove, their bodies moving lithely in the orange rays of the fast-falling sun.

Music was furnished by a group of older women, most of them boasting wrinkled faces and long, gray hair that hung to their waists, but their eyes were bright with the memories of their years as this pageant of Old Hawaii got under way.

One woman produced a heavy bass effect with a hollow gourd larger than her head, while others offered a strange, nostalgic memory by beating bamboo of varying lengths and thicknesses on the hard-packed earth. A more modern touch was offered by several guitars in the calloused hands of the ancients, who alternately strummed at the strings and beat out a pagan rhythm on the bodies of the instruments, while the dancers chanted the words of the ritual of a nearly forgotten time.

Suddenly the beat changed, growing more wild, and the music of the guitars seemed to take over the melody as the dancers scattered to the sidelines.

Malia whirled into the opening, wearing a skirt fashioned of *ti* leaves, which had been shredded and suspended from a band about her waist. Her breasts were held snuggly within the narrow bodice of a red cotton print.

A scarlet flower was tucked behind her left ear, its beauty and color heightened by the flow of black hair that fell unhampered below her shoulders. There was a necklace of sharks' teeth about her throat, and a band of the same about one ankle. Her head was thrown back and her teeth bared in a defiant smile as she began to dance in a strange, sensuous movement that seemed to set the entire circle of onlookers aflame.

The men shouted Polynesian words of encouragement to her as she danced like a demon released of its chains in hell, all of the pent-up emotions of a thousand generations working their way out in her motions. The women, too, screamed at her, feeling the hypnotic spell that she seemed to have cast.

As I stared at her, there was a slowly building ache in my groin and I glanced self-consciously at Hollman, who was looking on with a wide smile.

"Tahitian," he declared. "All of the Hawaiian royalty originally came from Tahiti."

The whiskey I had imbibed seemed to take hold, sinking to my loins, setting them afire, as I watched, and I recognized the dull ache as the pain of desire born of loneliness. But this was a sensation I had never felt before, and I wondered what the other men were thinking as I glanced about the circle of drunken faces. My gaze stopped on Drake Martin, who stood in the rear.

He had been in the act of rolling a cigarette, but he stood now with the tobacco-filled paper in his hand, the task forgotten as he stared toward the girl, his eyes bright with want.

As the dance ended, the girl whirled out of the circle and ran into the trees amid the cries of both men and women. Several young boys, barely in their teens, started to run after her but were called back by stern-voiced women.

"Mister Turk, I almost forgot to give this to you."

I turned to look at Kimo, who had pushed through the circle to kneel beside me. He held out a small, rectangular package which was bound neatly with cord.

"I got it in the mail yesterday and brought it back with the wagon last night," he explained earnestly. "It was in my pocket and I did not think of it until now."

I noticed that Martin had finished his cigarette and was lighting it as I ripped off the string and the paper that bound the box. Dropping them to my lap, I lifted the cover.

Inside was a layer of soft white cotton, and bedded in the exact center was a single bullet!

Eight

Kimo had been looking over my arm, and I knew he had seen the bullet before I clamped the top back on the box and pushed it into my shirt pocket, but Hollman turned to gaze at me curiously out of red-rimmed eyes.

"What's up, Sam?"

"Nothing." I shook my head. "Just a little Christmas gift from a friend back in the States."

His eyes swiveled back to the circle as several men came into the center of the clearing, laughing and shouting in Polynesian phrases, going into a comic hula routine. I picked up the wrapping to look at the postmark. I knew without looking that it had been mailed in Hilo.

It could have been that the raw, unaged liquor had hit me harder than I had expected, but I felt a strange satisfaction, knowing that Jeff Slack was my man. I had little doubt he was the one who had sent the bullet as a bizarre warning.

The months of waiting and wondering could be put behind me. The only thing I had to worry about now was Slack and staying out of his gunsights, being careful of which way my back was turned.

That thought sobered me for a moment, as I realized that the gunman would not be the type to offer warnings. Not if he really was intent upon killing someone. Instead, he would be more likely to bide his time, waiting until he could take advantage of darkness or try for a bushwhacking.

And if Slack should be the man who had tried to get me back in Texas, then followed me to Frisco, what was his reason?

The gunman was the only one who could answer that. Eventually he would, I promised. Hollman rose and lurched away toward the liquor supply as I turned to Kimo.

"Those times you saw Slack down in Hilo, Kimo. Was he wearing a gun?"

The Hawaiian boy frowned up at me out of dark eyes, thinking for a moment, then shaking his head.

"No, sir. I never see it." He hesitated, glancing away, then back to my face. "You think maybeso he make big *pilikia* by'mby?"

"Nothing like that," I said with an assurance I almost felt. "He won't bother us no more."

Malia had removed the grass skirt and reappeared from among the trees, picking her way through the seated crowd to where Martin still leaned against a tree. As I sat watching them, she stepped close to him, smiling and talking rapidly in low tones. The rider seemed embarrassed by what she said and looked away, his face showing no expression. As she went on, seeming to plead with him, he shook his head and turned to move away, disappearing into the gathering night.

While the girl stood looking after him I felt a vague stirring within me, recognizing it as a long-dormant emotion—jealousy. The ache of want was still with me, and I realized with a rush of misgivings that I resented the girl's obvious interest in the younger man.

It was crazy, I tried to tell myself. I was old enough to be the girl's father. But that didn't settle the uncomfortable emotion somewhere within.

"How about coming up to the office?" Hollman asked at my shoulder. As I turned to look at him inquiringly, he hoisted a gourd, shaking it so I could hear the sloshing noise, and grinned. "Got a couple of things I want to talk over with you without all this noise."

I nodded, and as we turned to go I nearly bumped into Himmler, who stood at the edge of the crowd, hands thrust deep in his pockets, watching the festivities with a stolid, blank expression, his eyes telling nothing through the thick lenses.

"Get in there and enjoy yourself," Hollman advised, clapping him on the back. "It's Christmas, man!"

A slight, almost apologetic smile brushed Himmler's lips and he nodded, saying nothing as Hollman brushed past him and I followed.

"God, I'm glad I only throw these things once a year," Mark groaned as he lit the coal-oil lamp and slid into his chair behind the cluttered desk. "There're going to be some real man-sized hangovers around this place come morning. How do you feel?"

Hollman wasn't as drunk as he pretended to be, I found, and the attitude of jovial friendship which he had displayed among the ranch employees dropped away like a mask.

"I'm fine. Been watching myself pretty close."

"Think you'll feel at all like doing some riding tomorrow?" he asked carefully. "We're short some cows."

"That's what you're paying me for. I'm listening."

He shook his head and took a drag from the gourd, passing it over the desk to me.

"Funny thing about these people," he said. "We've been lucky and got pretty dependable folks on the payroll, but some of these natives just sort of live from one *luau* to the next. They'll work long enough so they can get the money to throw a three or four-day party and invite all their friends. Then, when they're busted, they go back to work just long enough to finance another brawl.

"Anything's considered reason enough for a *luau*. A birth,

a death, a wedding, or just the plain damned ornery desire to get gawdawful drunk!"

I set the gourd on the edge of the desk, waiting for Hollman to light the pipe he had pulled from an ashtray.

"Felipe Montez came in last night to tell me we got nearly thirty head of prize heifers gone from the herd up at Kiluea. That's the bunch I've been saving for breeding stock when we get that new Hereford bull in from California."

"How long's it look like they've been gone?"

"Montez couldn't tell. Said he looked for the cows, then looked for sign, but if they'd drifted off, the rain washed out any tracks." He puffed at the pipe, exhaled smoke and tamped down the bowl with a pencil, frowning over his thoughts. "I don't reckon he looked too hard, of course. These boys don't much like prowling around that volcano. It's figured for real bad medicine. *Kapu.*"

"And you want me to go take a look? I've never been up on that part of the range but once."

"You can take Malia along with you. She knows the area, and it'll do her good to get away from the place for a day."

Recalling my feelings as I had watched her dance and later with Drake Martin, I knew I didn't want the girl near me. Not alone, at least.

"What about Kimo? Why can't I take him?"

Hollman shook his head, not looking at me. "Not him. He's scared stiff of the place. That's where his father got killed when he was still a baby. Got caught in a lava flow while he was trying to drive out part of the herd. What's left of him's still down under that volcanic glass, I reckon."

"I thought these volcanoes were supposed to be dead."

"I reckon a lot of other folks used to think so, too, but one goes on a rampage once in a while just to remind the Islanders that Pele can never die."

I was familiar with Polynesian mythology to the extent that I knew of Madame Pele, the goddess of fire, through my talks with Kimo. She was a very real part of local life,

Vengeance Is a Stranger

and this was particularly true of the boy. Her wrath had reached out to touch him personally.

"Them cows must be up there somewhere," Hollman declared fretfully. "Don't know where else they could be."

"*I* do."

He looked up warily. "Where?"

"The same place they'd be if some of them turned up missing in Texas."

"Naw, Sam. You got a lot to learn about these people." He shook the suggestion out of his head. "Maybe a beef now and then for food, and we expect that, but not thirty head."

"Maybe not," I told him, "but I'd be mighty suspicious of anyone that started putting on a lot of weight."

It was midmorning by the time Malia and I reached the high pasture, which was located on a flat bench just below the mammoth mass of lava rock and volcanic glass that had boiled down from the top of the mountain. At one time, the flat land also must have been of the same materials, but time and weather had reduced it to a fine enough texture to grow long-stemmed grass on which the cattle seemed to thrive.

I had been up before dawn, listening to the groans of some of the still-drunken *paniolos,* who tossed restlessly in their bunks. Joe Tam, the cook, had been up when I had awakened and was staggering about the lean-to kitchen, cursing softly as he fixed fried rice, steak and eggs for me.

Hollman had been right. There were going to be a lot of sore heads this day. He had been wise in giving them the time off in which to recover.

"How many head were supposed to be up here?" Malia wanted to know as we sat looking across the flat, grassy plain that flanked the lava heights.

"Just short of a hundred," I told her. There had been little talk between us during the ride from the ranch, for we had kept our animals at a steady jog all the way. I was looking forward to at least a part of the extra holiday, when we got back to the ranch, and I had set the pace.

She shook her head, frowning, as she surveyed the scattered grazing cattle. "Then Felipe was right. There's a lot less than that here now."

I glanced at her, recalling something my father had told me before he died. The mark of a good cattleman, he claimed, was one who could look at a herd and tell you at a glance the number of head within five.

The girl was dressed severely, wearing denim trousers and a heavy jacket against the cold of the higher elevation and the early-morning dampness. Her hair was tucked up sedately beneath her broad-brimmed hat, and there was nothing of the wild paganism that I had seen revealed the previous night at the *luau* and earlier at the *hukilau*. This day she was Mark Hollman's daughter. Nothing more.

But I couldn't keep back the memory of her twisting, tantalizing body as she had danced about the clearing, head back, smiling her enjoyment of her momentary freedom from care. It was a scene I knew I would never forget.

The mist had burned off of the high bench and together we counted the heifers, then began riding along the base of the lava flow, looking into hidden canyons for any sign of the missing animals. I looked for sign of tracks, too, on the trail leading down to another valley, but the heavy rains had blotted out any that might have been made, just as Hollman had suggested. It was noon before we had checked the entire area and we pulled up.

"They couldn't just fly away," Malia declared angrily, slapping a hand against her denim-clad leg. "They have to be here."

"Yeah. Unless someone wanted them somewhere else."

She ignored the comment, and I glanced upward toward the top of the volcano several thousand feet above us.

"What about up there?" I asked. "Anything to draw them on up the mountain?"

The girl shook her head. "Nothing. Nothing but rock and lava. Some caves. The lava tubes."

"Lava tubes? What're they?"

She shrugged, following my gaze. "The whole mountain is netted with them. Tunnels caused by bubbles in the lava when it hardened."

"We'd best take a look anyhow. Just a chance there might be some grass growing up there someplace."

"There isn't." She seemed a trifle angry that I would doubt her word. I went on as though I hadn't heard.

"There a trail leading up?"

"There is, but it's hard on horses. Besides, there isn't a thing up there to interest a cow."

"We'll look."

She seemed to hesitate for a moment, then offered another shrug, spurring her mount toward the dark formation.

The trail was narrow and wound back and forth across the face of the mountain. The floor had been washed by winter rains, dulling some of the sharp fragments, but still the lava was hard on the hooves of even a steel-shod horse. We had ridden less than five hundred yards when I realized that a cow would have too much native instinct to try such a climb for any enticement.

"Hold up," I called to the girl ahead of me, and she reined in her horse, turning in the saddle to look at me with a cynical smile.

"Satisfied?" she asked with heavy sarcasm. "Would you say that a cow might have more sense than you?"

I swung down from my own horse, staring at her for a moment. Then I strode forward, halting to look up at her.

"I'm listening," I told her. "There's something bothering you, and we might as well settle it. Maybe you didn't like the way I handled that thing with Jeff Slack. Maybe you'd have preferred that I didn't interfere at all!"

She wasn't looking at me. Instead, she seemed to be staring past me and into one of the black, jagged-mouthed caverns that faced onto the narrow, winding trail.

"Is that the answer?" I demanded, anger rising within me. Anger and frustration. "Or is it because Slack said I killed somebody? You've had a chip on your shoulder ever since that day!"

When the girl's eyes came down to glare at me, her hand suddenly slashed out with her quirt, and I ducked as the stinging leather whipped across my shoulder, cutting through the shirt with its pain.

The girl raised the whip again and I made a grab for it, but it was jerked out of my reach.

The sharp crack of a rifle sounded somewhere above, and at the same instant lava was sheared from a boulder a few inches from my head. Slivers of the black substance dug at my cheek.

The girl's horse screamed in terror, rearing against the sky, front feet pawing air. There was another shot that landed in the trail beneath my feet as the girl half fell from the saddle.

"Get under cover!" I screamed at her. She lay in the trail as her horse whirled and bolted, driving my own mount ahead of it. There was a third shot as I dived toward the girl, grabbing her and rolling her behind a protective ledge.

I lay there, breath coming from my lungs in huge gasps, my body half covering that of the girl. We were pressed into the recess in the rock as tightly as possible, while I looked upward, trying to locate the sniper's position, knowing at the same time that there was nothing I could do.

For a long time there was nothing but silence. Then I heard the clank of steel on rock somewhere below, and knew that our horses had not gone too far. A bird called somewhere, and on the tableland below us one of the cows began to bawl.

The minutes slipped by, each weighed with anxiety, and my ears were tuned to any sound that might tell of the approach of the sniper. Finally, I heard the creak of saddle leather above us, followed by the sound of a horse moving away among the rocks. It wasn't until the sound died away, leaving only the chirping of the bird, that I looked at the girl.

She had been stunned by the fall, but now she lay there quietly, looking up at me with strange, troubled eyes. The bitterness and anger of a few minutes before were gone, replaced by an expression I couldn't fathom.

"You're bleeding," she said quietly, almost whispering, as she reached up to run tender fingers across my cheek, where the lava particles had slashed it.

I lay there, looking into her eyes and realizing that this was not the daughter of my boss, but a woman who wore a flower over her left ear to signify she was unmarried and available.

Her fingers, light though the touch might have been, sent fire rippling over my skin, and that feeling of incompleteness born of desire came sweeping in like a piece of driftwood on a night tide.

I quit fighting myself then and dropped my lips to hers, disappointed at first at their lack of response, then gaining hope as they seemed to soften and I could feel the warmth of her mouth, tasting the pent-up love and emotion that I realized suddenly she had never allowed to be released.

Her hand slipped down to my shoulder, starting to push me away, then the fingers gripped the fabric, her nails biting through to my flesh.

Nine

Slowly I pulled away, ignoring the look of wonder and puzzlement that flitted across her face. I rose and stepped into the trail without looking back at her. The heat of passion of a few moments before had been chilled by practical realization.

"I'm sorry," I grunted at her. "Forgot myself for a minute. Drank too damned much of that *okolehao* yesterday, I reckon. Must still have plenty of it in me."

"You should apologize, when you just kept me from being shot?" she asked at my shoulder. I still didn't turn to look at her. "I should apologize for the way I've treated you, but I was afraid something like this would happen. Like the kiss."

She came around to look up into my face solemnly. "I've seen you looking at me."

"I said I was sorry. It won't happen again."

"How do you know, Sam? Perhaps I wanted it to happen. Isn't it possible that I want it to happen again?"

Her hands came up, starting to grip my shoulders, but I brushed them away, shaking my head, staring at her quiet, composed face. She meant what she said.

"Look, Malia. You don't know what you're saying. I'm nothing but a saddle tramp. You've probably guessed why I came here by now. I was running away from something. On top of all that, I know a little bit about how your father feels about you, and he's my friend. And I'm also old enough to be your father!"

It was a long speech, and I knew what I was doing to that feeling of loneliness as I said the words. I was only feeding future torment to that ache of want. She listened without a change of expression.

"My father was a saddle tramp, as you call it, when he came to the Islands," she said with that same quietness. "He is not ashamed of it, and he has done well."

"See if you can round up the horses." I pushed past her as I spoke. "I'm going to take a look." As I started up the trail, I heard her hesitate for a moment, then the sound of her boots scuffing against the rock.

The sniper had been hidden in a small hollow among the rocks and must have been watching us searching the bench below for some time. Half a dozen cigarette butts were scattered about. There also were three empty brass cartridges. I collected them, looking them over carefully. Each was a .30-30 rifle shell.

I glanced up at the sound of steel ringing on rock. Malia came around a turn in the trail, leading the two horses. She dropped the reins and came forward, glancing over the ground, seeing the cigarette butts, then noticing the shells I held in my hand. She reached out to take one, looking at the numbered manufacturer's identification.

"He could have killed us both," she said softly, looking up at me.

"He?"

"Whoever it was! You don't think I know—"

"Certainly not," I apologized, "but I don't think whoever it was wanted to hit you. Maybe he wasn't even trying for me. He might just have been trying to scare us away."

"That kind of proves what happened to the cattle, though, doesn't it?"

"In my book it does, but your father may not think so. He's

convinced none of the folks around here would go in for wholesale rustling."

"Rustling?" The word was strange to her.

"Stealing. When someone steals a batch of horses or cattle."

"Oh."

I turned and started to mount, but she tugged at my shoulder. She was frowning, looking at the ground, as she said hesitantly, "Sam. What happened a while ago down there"—her eyes came up to look at me slowly—"was as much my fault as yours."

I nodded slowly. "Yeah. I know." She stiffened at my words, anger starting to rise in her eyes. "Like you said, things like that can happen. I'm a man and you're a woman, but you'd better pick someone your own age. What about young Martin?"

Her eyes narrowed for a moment, and I knew that I had struck a sore point. She looked away, speaking softly.

"I don't know, Sam. He's so strange. Sometimes I think he loves me and that I love him. Other times we're strangers. It's as though he had just come from San Francisco and we are strangers, meeting again for the first time. I don't understand him at all."

It wasn't hard to understand what she meant. I had the same feeling about the boy ever since he had come to the ranch.

"Do you think you love him now? After what almost happened? Between *us*, I mean."

She still didn't look at me, but shook her head. "I don't know. Maybe I just wanted to hurt him. Get him out of my mind. And was trying to use you as an instrument to do it."

"Or maybe you were trying to hurt yourself!"

Her dark eyes flashed to me, surprise brightening them at my comment, but I turned back to my horse, leaving her to mount by herself. She said nothing all the way to the ranch, and it was dark when we arrived, and I took her horse at the corral.

"Are you going to tell my father what happened?" she asked.

"If I didn't, you would, wouldn't you?"

"I mean about the man shooting at us." She hesitated, starting to look away, then keeping her eyes on mine with a visible effort. "About the other, I will tell him nothing. Perhaps I was trying to hurt myself, as you said. There is no reason to hurt him, too."

"No," I decided slowly. "There's no reason for that, but I'll have to tell him about the bushwhacking try."

"Bushwhacking?"

"The man that tried to shoot us—if that's what he was up to." I was thinking that, with three tries and a rifle, someone was a pretty bad shot.

I could barely see her dark face in the night, but her teeth were bright and her eyes flashed as she took a step closer to me.

"I have been thinking about what happened up there. With us, I mean," she said softly, hesitating. "Thank you, Sam, for not taking me when you had the chance."

"I don't think it would have been right for either one of us," I told her gruffly. I was lying even to myself, but it was in the past now. It would always be in the past.

"No," she said in the same soft tone. "Not for either of us."

She turned and disappeared in the darkness toward the house, while I turned the horses into the corral and hung the bridles and saddles on the top rail of the enclosure. The stars were shining, but they seemed a little less bright as I walked toward the light that burned in the office. I was tired, the weariness going beyond anything physical. Time had made an old man of me. Not my years of life, but the years in prison. The time I had been robbed of. As I walked through the night, I knew that it was too late to cure the loneliness now. It was something that would always be with me, a ghost that would sit on the end of my bed at night, invading my dreams. Clinging to my shoulder by day.

I had come to the Islands to escape the past and whoever it was out of that past that still pursued me. I had come with a dream of starting a new life. Instead, I was only beginning a new existence. There is a wide difference.

The hallway was dark, and somewhere I heard a door shut as I came into the ranch house, but at the end of the corridor I saw the light burning beneath the door leading to Hollman's office.

I knocked on the door, then pushed it open. Himmler turned toward me, scowling in the lamplight. In his hands he held the .30-30 carbine which had hung on the wall behind Mark's desk!

The muzzle of the rifle dropped and he started to speak, but I was across the room in a bound, knocking the muzzle aside and driving a fist into his mouth. His thick-lensed spectacles went flying and he sagged against the wall, as the weapon dropped from his slack grip.

He tried to speak again, his mouth forming words, but I battered them away, my fists pounding against his parted lips. Then he started to whirl away, and I moved to block him. A bony knee came upward, driving toward my groin, but I sensed the move and twisted to catch it on the inside of my thigh. The force sent me driving back across the room, slamming into the door.

Himmler dropped to his knees, grabbing for the rifle, but I dived at him, throwing him away, and as we rolled over and over on the floor, one of the chairs spilled against the wall with a heavy clatter.

One of the man's thin thumbs found my eye and tried to gouge it, driving pain along the nerves into my head. I swore at him as he babbled curses and obscenities in my ear, his breath coming in deep, fearful gasps.

I slammed a fist across his chin and jerked his hand away from my face at the same time. There was strength in his thin frame, but I outweighed him by thirty pounds.

"Take a shot at me, you dirty bastard!" I shouted in his ear. "I've been waiting for the day I found out who you were!"

Suddenly he brought his knee driving upward into my stomach, and I was sent catapulting over his head, my face smashing into the wall. As I rolled over, he was scrambling to his feet, the rifle clubbed in his hands, his chest heaving, and his weak eyes glancing wildly about.

I had the feeling I was going to be sick, but it was the sickness of elation. I knew now who it was that had been dogging my trail ever since the day I had walked out of the gates at Huntsville!

"Why, Himmler!" I graveled at him through my own panting breath. "Why do you want to kill me?"

Uncertainty came into his face for an instant as he stared at me, but his grip tightened on the carbine.

"I'm going to kill *you* instead, but I want to know why you've been following me. Why?"

I took a step toward him and he swung at me, the rifle stock missing by only a hair as I dodged back. He screamed as I closed on him, knocking the weapon away, then grabbing him by the shirt with my left hand. Slowly I began to drive blows into his face, and felt his knees buckle beneath his own weight.

"Why? Why did you come here?" I realized dimly that I was screaming, but my tones seemed muffled in my ears. "Why did you want to kill me? Talk, you back-shooting bastard!"

He gurgled through the blood in his mouth and tried to speak, but couldn't. His eyes were glazed with pain and puzzlement. As I dropped him, he lay in a heap, shuddering, his face buried in his arms. I pushed a toe into his ribs, wanting to hurt him, wanting him to scream, but he didn't move.

He was quietly crying, seemingly unmindful that I stood over him.

There was a sound in the hallway and I looked up as Mark Hollman swung the door open, a lamp in his hand, and froze, his face twisted in horror at the scene.

"It's him," I told him through my spent curtain of emotion. "This is the bastard's been trying to kill me!"

"Turk, you're a fool!" Mark Hollman's voice was low, almost hidden in his chest, a sound resembling a moan. "I thought you'd changed, but you're still a kill-crazy fool!"

My breathing stopped, and the red curtain of anger that had blanketed my brain for a few moments seemed to hang for an instant, then melt away. On the floor at my feet the bookkeeper stirred, muttering something as he tried to sit up. Mark Hollman stared at me with open revulsion, his face twisted into a mask of dislike in the lamplight. Behind him I could see Malia's frightened face. Hollman turned to her.

"Get some water and towels. Hurry up!"

He came into the room, setting the lamp on the table beside the other one, and bent to grab Himmler beneath the shoulders, not looking at me.

"Help me get him in a chair," he growled. "Show you're good for something besides trying to kill people!"

"But he tried to kill me!" I shouted at him. "He almost shot your daughter!"

"Shut up and help me!" he ordered.

I grabbed one of the man's arms and helped push him into the chair beside the desk. Malia came into the room and put a bowl on the table, laying a folded cloth beside it. She looked at me with a scowl, and then at Mark. She was about to speak as her father turned on her.

"Get out of here!" he ordered roughly. "And don't say anything to anyone. Not even to Toshiko!" Toshiko was the ancient Japanese housekeeper.

Hollman wet the cloth and pushed the bookkeeper's lolling head back with his hand cupped under the man's chin. Himmler was conscious, but his eyes were still closed as the ranch manager tenderly wiped the blood away from his mouth and nostrils. More blood trickled down his chin from a cut lip, and Hollman pressed the towel over it for a moment.

"You'd have killed him if I hadn't heard you," Hollman muttered.

"I meant to kill him! He tried to kill me!" My voice was a snarl. "I walked in here and he was standing with the carbine aimed right at me!"

"He was cleaning it, you fool! I told him to!"

Hollman turned to stare at me, waiting for me to dispute the statement. Slow realization broke over me. Standing there, looking down at the broken face, I felt naked, stripped.

"My glasses," the man whined, pain riding the words. "Are they broken?"

Dumbly I walked to the corner where they had fallen and picked them up, handing them to Mark. He looked at them in the flickering light, then pushed them into Himmler's hand. Still not opening his eyes, the bookkeeper put them on, carefully adjusting the earpieces. When he looked through the heavy lenses, his eyes were on my face. His eyes were narrowed to hatred-filled slits, and I felt a chill creeping through my innards.

"Remind me not to clean any more rifles, Mister Hollman," he said thinly. "At least, not while this madman is in the vicinity."

"But someone took a shot at us. Three of them!" I dug into my shirt pocket and extended my hand so both of them could see the empty shell casings I had picked up on the volcano. "When I walked in on him he was standing there with the carbine. What else could I think?"

Hollman said nothing, staring at me with a flat, dull look in his eyes.

"But why would I want to kill you?" the bookkeeper asked, lisping the words over his torn lips. I looked down at him. The sickness I had felt during the fight was a heavy, sodden weight of shame resting in my stomach.

"Someone tried to kill me just before I left Texas," I told him slowly. "It's been tried since."

"That doesn't explain why *I* should try," the man insisted quietly. "Why?"

I shook my head, looking away. "I don't know," I told him wearily. My hands were shaking, and I clenched them to hide it. "I don't know why anyone would want to."

"There's something perhaps you should know about my past," Himmler said, the tone coated with irony. "I was not in a position to kill you until four days before I sailed from San Francisco."

"Shut up, Himmler," Mark growled, turning toward him. "You don't owe him any explanations."

The bookkeeper didn't look at him. Instead, he grinned at me, his lips twisted into a sneer. His tone was chiding as he said, "But I want Mister Turk to know. I was in a military prison until I came here. I had been there for five years!"

I stiffened at the mention of prison, and he smiled more broadly, seeming to take pleasure in the effect his statement had on me. He nodded, as though to accept my surprise.

"You don't owe him any explanation," Hollman repeated. "You didn't try to kill him. That's enough for him to know."

Himmler ignored him as though he hadn't heard. His eyes were still on me, as he went on. "I was an Army paymaster, Sam. A major. Then, one day, my accounts were short. I thought I could cover it, and I was wrong.

"I told Mister Hollman about it in a letter which a friend arranged to mail for me from prison. He needed a bookkeeper, and I needed a new start. Any questions that doesn't answer?"

The story was told with a precise politeness that made it sound like an often-repeated formal confession. I looked away, shaking my head.

"Sorry," I mumbled. "I owe you an apology."

"That ain't going to help him heal any sooner," Hollman charged.

"Apology accepted," the bookkeeper said softly. "In your spot, I might have done the same thing."

Hollman put the bowl and the towel back on the desk and turned to me.

"If you'd reported to me first, maybe this could've been avoided," he said. I started to interrupt, to tell him that I had thought he was in the office, but he waved me into silence.

"You were right about them missing heifers," he said, scowling. "Kimo came riding in tonight with a hide across his saddle. His dog found it buried in a gully. There were a bunch more of them there, too. Almost thirty. Someone's been butchering my cows!"

"Have any ideas?" I asked quietly, still feeling Himmler's eyes on my face.

"None. I don't know anyone around here that would do it." He tilted his head to look at me suspiciously. "Do you?"

"Maybe." I nodded slowly. "Whoever it was must have been about to cut out some more stock, when Malia and I showed up this morning."

Hollman took a step toward me, the scowl darkening his face. His voice was low and heavy as he said, "Whoever it is, I want it stopped. Understand? Stopped!"

I nodded.

"Stopped without a gun," he added. "That's for you!"

I nodded again, wondering if he knew what he was asking. A man could get real dead trying to follow an order like that.

Ten

"Mister Himmler, he is a bad man?" Kimo asked me thoughtfully, looking straight ahead down the trail as we approached the outskirts of Hilo.

I looked at the Hawaiian boy in surprise. "No. He's not bad. Why do you ask a fool question like that?"

He shrugged, still looking straight ahead. "I was outside window last night when you hit him. You hit him plenty hard. Mmm!" He jabbed at the air to illustrate his point. "I hear him say him in prison. Must be bad man."

"What the hell were you doing outside that window?" And I was wondering how much the hands at the ranch would know about the fracas as a result. Hollman and I had agreed that nothing was to be said about the matter to anyone.

"Just walking past," the boy explained innocently. "Hear big noise and look in. Big fight." He turned to look at me with the seriousness of youth, shaking his head. "I no think I want to fight you ever, Mister Turk. You fight too hard!"

"It was nothing," I assured him. "Mister Himmler and I just had a little trouble. It's all over now."

I had started out early from the ranch, explaining to the *paniolos* that Hollman was sending me into Hilo to run an errand. I was less than a mile from the corral when Kimo had overtaken me, explaining that he was going for the mail.

"True some *haole* man try to shoot you yestiday?" he went on, eyes flicking back to the trail. "Somebody try, maybeso you better carry gun. Shoot back next time."

"Where would I get a gun?" My tone was sharper than I meant it to be. "The boss doesn't allow them."

"Oh, you have gun. I know," he declared. "See gun in your bag."

I pulled up my mount and reached out to grab his bridle. A sudden suspicion knifed through me. "What were you doing in my stuff?"

The boy looked at me, drawing back, eyes suddenly flickering with fear. "No mean it, Mister Turk. 'Mistake,' I think you say."

"Answer me! What were you doing in my bag?"

"Tam-san, he tell me to clean up bunkhouse one day. I sweep out and move around bags of all *paniolo* fellers. See piece of shirt sticking out of yours. Open up to put shirt back in. See gun. I not touch!"

He made the speech rapidly, as though trying to get it out before I should make up my mind about something. He shook his head vigorously. "I not touch!" he repeated. "Not any."

"You tell anyone about the gun?" I asked. He shook his head, and I released the bridle.

"I hear Mister Hollman tell you to find cow stealer," he went on. "Maybeso you need gun now."

"As far as you're concerned, I don't have one," I told him shortly. "Understand?"

"I understand. You no have gun. I never see it."

I spurred my mount to a trot as we hit the main thoroughfare and the boy turned in before the post office. I rode on through the town and down to the waterfront, finding the pier where my ship had tied up when I had arrived.

A ship was being loaded and I watched for a time, as huge logs of *koa* wood were swung up by cables and tied down on the deck. I stayed more than an hour, watching until the hatches were covered and the workers on the wharf began to cast off. As the laborers began to clear away, collecting their pay from an elderly Chinese wearing a black robe and a queue down his back, I pushed through them to wait until the man was alone.

I questioned him about the ship, her destination and her cargo, but learned nothing. At least, not what I was after. I moved on along the waterfront, asking more questions of Chinese businessmen, dock workers and seamen. Most eyed me with open suspicion, even when I twiddled currency in my hands, creasing and uncreasing it. Either they knew nothing, or they didn't believe in bribery. Not from me, at least.

It was noon by the time I had worked my way around the harbor's lip to the other main wharf—the one where the ship on which Slack, Martin and Himmler had arrived was tied up. There was no vessel now, though, and it was deserted except for an aged Hawaiian who lolled in the sun, a sleeping dog beside him.

He looked up groggily as I walked toward him, my heels vibrating on the splintered planks. The dog raised its head, growled at me, looked to its master for instructions, then went back to sleep when there were none.

I asked the old man the same questions I had asked all along the harbor, and he ran his hand through his kinky, white hair, thoughtfully eying the money in my hand. He smelled of rum and his eyes were red, his face bloated. He had been sitting on a wooden crate, and I had a hunch there was a bottle hidden beneath it. The look in his eyes as he eyed the bills in my hand was evidence, though, that the bottle was about empty.

Several boats had tied up there during the week, he admitted. One had sailed shortly before dawn, just as he had come on duty to guard the warehouses. Not that anyone would pilfer from them, but the owners insisted upon a guard, and, after all, it was a job that required long hours but little actual labor.

The ship that had sailed? It had been a Chinese ship bound for San Francisco carrying silks and spices. Provisions? Yes, they had taken provisions aboard. The last things loaded. Mostly rice, but there had been two sides of beef.

Two of the Chinese seamen had brought the meat to the pier in a hired wagon, but he had seen the ship's captain pay another man for it. A *paniolo* by his dress, but a *haole* like myself.

The old man shrugged wearily as I asked for a description of the white man. It had been so dark and he was still a little drunk. It hadn't mattered, so he hadn't looked too closely. No one would steal anything from the warehouses. What would there be inside that a *paniolo* would want?

As I paid him, he grinned happily, turning over the box and bringing up the gourd of native whiskey, asking that I join him in a drink. He didn't really mean it, since the sloshing meant the container was nearly empty, but now he had the means of procuring more. The day was starting well.

He called his thanks after me as he stood leafing the money, and I turned to walk back along the wharf to where I had left my horse.

The Golden Dragon was hidden on a side street, and I found it only after asking directions of a Hawaiian boy who was playing in the street. It was located in a dilapidated frame structure that undoubtedly had not seen a coat of paint since it was built, and the roof had once been of shingles, but had been covered over with palm thatch as the shakes had splintered beneath countless years of rain and sun.

There was a large plate-glass window on each side of the single door. These had been painted to shoulder height with black paint, and carelessly lettered across each of them was the name of the establishment. The door was covered by strings of Chinese beads which were meant to keep out the flies and to offer semiprivacy, but as I pushed through the rattling curtain I noticed that both efforts had failed.

A three-piece native orchestra stood on a small platform at the rear of the narrow, deep room, playing listlessly, while a young native girl clad only in an abbreviated sarong performed an equally uninspired hula.

A dozen tables were scattered about the floor, but most of the customers, all apparently seamen or beachcombers, were lined up at the bar, the majority staring into their drinks rather than at the entertainment.

The place seemed dark after the brightness outside, and I hesitated for a moment before making my way to the bar, where the Chinese bartender waited expectantly. I pointed to a bottle of Scotch on the back bar, and he turned to pick it up, wiping off the gathered dust with a dirty apron. He pushed an equally grimy glass before me and filled it as I threw some coins on the bar. Several of the seamen had looked up curiously as I entered but went back to their own thoughts. The buzz of low conversation hung over the bar as I raised the drink and turned to look around.

Jeff Slack was seated at a table at the far side of the room, his back toward me. A nearly empty bottle was before him and he was playing idly with a pile of gold pieces, stacking them into small piles. I downed half the drink and realized why the bottle had seen such little use. The Scotch had been cut with native whiskey. I gagged against the mixture and turned to eye the bartender, who was watching with evident interest. Seeing my expression, he grinned and turned away to another customer with a shrug.

The music ended and the musicians put down their instruments, heading for the bar, while the Hawaiian girl moved across the floor, making her way between the scarred tables to where Slack was waiting. He glanced up at her, then nodded toward a chair. The girl's eyes went to the stack of gold pieces in front of him. Her voice was low and anxious, but I was able to hear the words.

"Is there enough, Jeff? Enough for us to leave this place? To go to San Francisco?" She spoke with careful diction obviously learned at one of the mission schools. She was frowning wistfully as she spoke, apparently on her best behavior with the gunman.

"Not yet." He pushed over the stack of coins and they rang musically on the table top. "Pretty soon now."

"But how soon? That's what you keep saying." She lowered her head, allowing the hair to fall away from her shoulders to hide her features. "I must get away from this place, Jeff. I hate it! I hate everyone here, and they hate me!"

"Shut up!" he growled at her. "Quit talking like that!"

She looked up, her face twisted with emotion, tears in her eyes. Some of the mission training left her voice as she went on. "But it is true! I have broken a *kapu!* It is wrong to dance for money. The hula is religious to my people. My own mother says I must have been sired by a demon!"

Jeff Slack reached across the table to slap the girl across the face. She drew back, staring at him with surprise and a show of suddenly realized fear. He poured himself another drink as he spoke to her in low, harsh tones.

"You listen to me, girl, and listen good! I said I'd take you back with me, but you're going to do exactly as I tell you until we have enough money." He lifted the drink and downed it, then waved to the gold coins with the empty glass. "This may look like a lot of dough to you, but it wouldn't get us to Frisco and keep us for even a week. We have to have more. A lot more!"

The girl hesitated, frowning at him, then nodded slowly. "I will do as you say. I will talk to the sailors and tell them where they can buy meat for their ships more cheaply than in the town."

Slack didn't hear me approaching, but the girl looked up at me, still frowning, uncertainty flitting across her features. She could have been pretty, but her hair had been curled too often, losing its natural luster. The lipstick that was a dark streak across her mouth looked unnatural, and the rouge on her cheeks had been applied inexpertly, giving her a painted-doll look.

Slack saw the expression on her face and started to turn as I threw the bullet on the table before him. It was the one that had been mailed to me from Hilo. He whirled on the chair, freezing.

"I'm making you a little trade, Slack. I appreciate the gift, but I'm giving it back to you. All it costs is Hollman's money there."

He glared up at me, eyes flat and red around the yellow, dead-looking pupils. His nostrils dilated nervously as he brought his eyes down to my hip, looking for a gun. I had noticed that he wasn't wearing one when I first spotted him.

"What're you talking about?" he demanded. "I worked for that money." His eyes flicked to the bullet on the table. "And I don't know what you mean about the bullet."

"No? Then maybe it'll give you something to think about on that trip back to Frisco." I reached past him to scoop up the gold. The coins were Chinese, bearing strange characters and each with a hole through its exact center.

Slack leaped to his feet, his chair going over behind him, clattering on the floor like an anvil in a funeral parlor. All talk in the place had stopped, and I knew, without looking, that the men lined up at the bar were watching. Slack made a grab for my hand holding the money, but I blocked him with an elbow.

"You're crazy, Turk! You can't just walk in here and take my money away from me. No one can!"

"I'm not taking it," I told him calmly. It might have been the mixture of Scotch and the native stuff that had done it, but I was calm, watching him for any move. The girl slid back her chair, its legs screeching on the board floor, then stood up, looking warily from the gunman to me, then back again. Fear magnified her eyes.

"You might say I'm collecting," I went on. "Collecting for Mark Hollman. He appreciates your work, though, and he always pays his bills. Here!"

I threw half a dozen gold coins on the table, and his eyes shot toward them, then back to me.

"I'm going to kill you, Turk!" he hissed.

"Don't press your luck. You didn't do so well with that rifle up on the volcano yesterday."

"I'll kill you if it's the last thing I do."

"I don't think so." Perhaps the threat should have frightened me, but it didn't. After all the months of terror, not knowing from where death might strike, it was easy to face him. "There's a ship pulling out of here tonight for the States. You'll be on it or Mark Hollman will swear out a warrant for your arrest. There's enough gold there to pay your passage."

He stared at me for a long moment, then the stiffness seemed to go out of his spine and his shoulders drooped. He looked away, to the gold on the table, then to the face of the girl.

"You must take me with you, Jeff," she whispered, desperation in her voice. "You said you would take me."

"Take you, hell!" he shouted at her. "How far do you think both of us would get on that kind of money?"

She stared at him for an instant before her head dropped and she started to crumple, grasping the back of the chair for support.

"Be on that ship!" I told him and started to turn away. I heard a movement behind me, and there was a surprised gasp from someone at the bar.

I whirled aside as Slack launched himself at me, the whiskey bottle, raw liquor pouring from the mouth, swinging toward my face.

Eleven

Off balance, I dodged, trying to avoid the bottle, but it crashed down upon my shoulder with numbing force, shattering. The jagged glass neck clawed along my left arm, sending fire shooting along my biceps.

Slack recoiled with the speed of a snake preparing for another strike, drawing the glass fang backwards, then lunging at my face. The girl screamed with a terror-wrought wail as I leaped back and aimed a kick at his groin.

The toe of my boot overshot and caught him low in the stomach, driving him back and sending pain rocketing up into his face to distort the smile of conquest which had rested there for a second. His arm dropped, but he still held the glass weapon as he whirled away swiftly, doubling over to regain his breath.

His hip struck the table and it toppled over, the gold pieces scattering toward the bar. With a whoop, one of the beachcombers dived for one of them. Others began scrambling about the floor, upsetting chairs in their rush for the Chinese money.

I leaped toward the gunman, but he kicked a chair in front of me and I went crashing over it, twisting to catch the impact on my left shoulder. The action sent pain shooting through the torn muscles of my arm.

Slack shrieked a charge in a high-pitched woman's scream

as he dived for me, but I kicked the chair at him and he went down, the bottle neck shattering on the floor.

We came up together and, as I closed with him, he whirled, trying for the door. My foot shot out, sending the overturned chair skidding across the uneven floor in front of him. He swore as he catapulted over it, kicking viciously in an attempt to clear it from his way. He landed full on his face amid the remains of the broken whiskey bottle, and a scream of pain went up from the floor.

He rolled over, threshing about in an effort to clear the glass particles from his face. There was a deep cut along one cheek, and blood formed a rivulet, dripping from his chin. The girl screamed again, louder and more shrilly, as I stepped over the chair and reached down to grab him.

The glass had carved a future scar from the corner of his mouth almost to the point of his chin, and the pink flesh was laid bare. He was whimpering with pain as he came to his feet, my hand clutching the front of his shirt. He pawed at me weakly, trying to push me away. As he shook his head, mumbling, flecks of blood polka-dotted my shirt front.

"Don't, Turk!" he whined almost incoherently. "I'll leave! I'll leave and never come back!" His hands were still waving weakly before him, like those of a ghost trying its first materialization.

I pushed him into a chair and he slumped there, his hands over his face to cover the wounds as he began to sob. Blood ran down his wrists, turning his cuffs scarlet.

The girl, her face pale beneath her natural coloring, stood behind one of the tables that had not been overturned in the melee. Her mouth was open, eyes bugged. She was extremely ugly at that moment. As I stepped toward her, she gasped in terror and took a step backward.

"I'm giving you a job," I told her through my own heavy breathing, as I dug into my pocket with my good hand. "Get him to a doctor and get that face sewed up."

She nodded dumbly as I threw more of the Chinese gold

pieces on the table before her. Her eyes stayed on my face, taking no interest in the money.

"Then, see that he's on that ship that's leaving the harbor tonight, even if he has to stay on the deck. There should be enough there to pay you for your trouble, too. Understand?"

She nodded again, her eyes finally dropping to the money, and muttered something in the Polynesian dialect that I didn't understand.

Weakness was invading my knees as I turned toward the door. Blood was dripping from my own fingertips, and my entire sleeve had turned dark red. I clenched my hand to be certain that no vital muscles had been slashed. The action sent pain driving up my arm, and yellow spots danced before my eyes as I made for the bead-curtained door.

As I reached the entrance, I heard steps behind me and turned, reaching out for the door frame as a support. It wasn't Slack, who still sat on the chair, rocking back and forth and sobbing softly, while blood puddled the floor in front of him. It was the girl. The fear was gone from her face and she smiled at me with a friendliness that was evidence of her profession—or of her sideline, at least.

"*Paniolo,*" she said, extending her hand with opened palm to display the gold pieces. "I must ask your help. If Jeff-san leaves, I must leave with him. I am *kapu,* an outcast, among my own people. He is all that I have." She glanced down at the money, shaking it in her palm until the pieces clinked together.

"There is not enough money for both of us to go." Her voice was soft and enticing, almost making a promise. "He promised to take me with him."

"Do you know Mark Hollman?" I asked gruffly. She nodded, tilting her head to one side in puzzlement, but still holding the smile.

"I have seen him many times."

"Then you should know he ain't running a charity institution. You're on your own."

She allowed the smile to drop away and she snarled at me, starting to move closer, but I shouldered her out of the way with my bad arm. There was a smear of blood on the band of cotton print that covered her bosom as I swept aside the Chinese beads and stepped into the street. I glanced back and saw her trying to rub the stain away with one hand, the other clutching the gold pieces. She was muttering Polynesian curses beneath her breath.

The bartender had come from behind the bar with a wet towel and was trying to hold it over Jeff Slack's face, but the gunman pushed him away, cursing him through his splintered mouth.

Jeff-*san*, the girl had called him. It was a Japanese term, *san* being a word of highest esteem and respect when placed after a person's name. I staggered dizzily down the street, holding my upper arm to keep back the flow, laughing to myself. The sound was dim in my ears and seemed to come through the pounding of heavy surf, but I found it immensely funny.

Jeff-san! An indication of esteem and respect! He'd be dead in hell before anyone held him in any kind of esteem with the scarred face that was going to be his! And I could lead the kind of life I had hoped to when I came to the Islands. No more fears. No more staring into the night, nerves dodging at shadows, wondering whether The One was there!

I was still laughing when I found the small, hand-lettered sign on the main street that announced the office of Dr. Leonard Simpson. It was a small, recently painted frame building with a New England air about it, but I barely noticed as I stumbled up the steps and kicked at the door, not releasing my hold on the injured arm. Most of the flow of blood had stopped, but I was afraid it would start again if the pressure was released.

There was no sound for a moment, and I kicked again, swearing loudly. Footsteps echoed within, and a moment later a tall, middle-aged woman with graying hair and sunken cheeks stared out at me, taking in the sight. Her expression didn't change as she turned to call over her shoulder, then stepped aside, jerking her head in indication that I should enter.

"Leonard! Leonard, you have a patient!" she called, then nodded to a wooden bench against the wall. The entire room was painted white, as were the few furnishings. In one corner stood an instrument case with a glass door revealing the array of chrome-plated surgical tools. In another corner was an operating table.

The doctor came in, a tall, thick man with watery eyes and a whiskey-veined nose, who wore his shirtsleeves rolled above his elbows to reveal dead-white arms which ended in long, tapering fingers. His hair was ruffled as though he had just awakened, and he was putting on a pair of gold-rimmed spectacles as he looked at me critically.

"Oh, Lord," he said wearily. "I don't have to ask where you've been!"

I grunted something incoherent at him and he came forward, the tiredness still in his voice despite the accusing tone. "They ought to close that Golden Dragon. You're the third I've had this week." He jerked a head at his wife and she closed in from the other side, while he grabbed my arm roughly and ripped the sleeve up the middle. I flinched, cursing as the fabric was torn away from the wound and the woman grabbed both of my shoulders, her thumbs digging into my neck muscles.

He was grinning cynically as he tore the sleeve away from the rest of the shirt, inspecting the wound through the blood. He glanced at his wife and jerked his head toward a table which supported an array of bottles. She released her grip and turned to pick up a rectangular bottle of brown glass and hand it to him with a pad of clean cotton that she took from a white enameled container.

"The other one still alive, or will he be coming along,

too?" he asked sarcastically. He daubed at the wound with the cotton, and the alcohol burned deep into the wound.

I stiffened involuntarily, growling, "That make you the only doctor in town?"

"Not the only one, but the cheapest. All the bums that get half-killed in that glorified opium den turn up here to be put back together."

"I can pay my bill," I snapped at him. "You just put the arm together like you're bragging."

The sound of pounding surf was heavy in my ears and his white shirt before me turned gray, the room starting to grow dark.

"He's going to pass out," his wife warned shrilly.

"No wonder," he explained mildly. "He's been bleeding like a castrated elephant!"

I felt his hand on my shoulder, helping me up as he asked in a more kindly tone, "Think you can make it over here to the table and stretch out?"

I nodded dumbly, stumbling against him as I tried to walk. The woman grabbed me under the good arm, and they half carried me to the operating table, where I sat down heavily, watching the corner of the room near the ceiling bob up and down. One of them lifted my feet up, turning me, and hands pushed me down flat on the table.

"You want some morphine before you start to sew him up?" the woman's voice said from a long way off.

"No use to waste it," he replied. "He isn't going to feel anything. He's out now." And I knew he was right, as blackness closed in over me.

It was night when I awoke, and I lay there for a long time staring up at the dancing shadows on the ceiling. At first, I didn't know where I was, then I recalled the fight and staggering through the street, natives staring at me and drawing back as I made my way to the doctor's office.

And the dream flashed through my mind. Jeff Slack kept

bobbing in front of me, slashing me with the jagged bottle neck, taking his time, enjoying it, while the girl stood behind him, laughing.

Each time he carved a piece out of my flesh with the weapon she shook her hands, clinking pieces of gold together, screaming, "Not enough! I go with Jeff-san! Not enough money!"

Slack was smiling as he worked on me, smiling through a blanket of blood caused by two tremendous cuts on his face. The pain didn't seem to bother him at all as he kept after me, taking a step each time I did, keeping the short distance always between us, slashing at me, while he kept repeating over and over, "I'm going to kill you, Turk. Kill you. I came a long way. Now I'm going to kill you!"

His monotone had been punctuated by the laughter from the girl, and the men at the bar kept picking gold pieces off the floor, buying new drinks with them and shouting encouragement to the gunman, laughing each time he scored with the broken bottle.

I shuddered uncontrollably at the recollection and heard a sound that resembled a sob. It took a moment to realize it had risen from my own chest.

I tried to sit up, and pain coursed along my arm. I looked to find that it had been heavily bandaged from elbow to shoulder. I moved it gingerly and felt the stitches pulling at the flesh underneath. Mark Hollman was going to be more than unhappy when he heard about this! Yet, I tried to assure myself, he had ordered me to stop the rustling, and I had stopped it. At least, I had stopped Jeff Slack!

I looked up at the sound of heels on the bare floor, and the doctor entered, a tumbler in his hand. There was half an inch of liquor in the bottom of it. The rest and more, I could see, was in him. He was slightly drunk.

"How's the patient?" he asked thickly, beaming at me through gold-rimmed glasses. "Didn't expect you to wake up before morning."

"Got to see a boat off," I told him. "What time is it?"

"Almost ten o'clock. Why don't you lay down there and stay the night. Don't cost you no more."

I shook my head and slipped my feet over the edge of the operating table, standing up. My knees still felt weak from the loss of blood, but I was in better shape than I had expected to find myself.

"Got to move," I told him. "What do I owe you?"

"For patching you up or for saving your life?" He was grinning at the question, satisfied with his own humor. "You almost got knifed again while I was working on you."

I couldn't help staring at him. "What happened?"

"Some girl, the one that works down at that Golden Dragon, brought your friend in. He took one look at you and wanted to finish the job he started." He hesitated and took a sip out of the glass, rolling the liquor over his tongue before allowing it to slide down his throat. "Had to tell her to find him another doctor. Wouldn't do to have both of you here under the same roof. Whichever one of you came out of it first would've been the live one. That's all he could say"—the surgeon went on thoughtfully, some of the drunkenness going out of his eyes—"that he was going to kill you. The girl kept insisting he had to catch a boat. That the boat you're talking about?"

I nodded dumbly, looking at my shirt. I could hardly go wandering around the streets looking like that. The doctor saw and stepped forward to look at me more closely.

"Tell you what," he offered. "I got a shirt you can wear, if you'll bring it back the next time you're in town. You work for the Parkers?"

I shook my head. "Mark Hollman."

His eyes widened a trifle. "Understood he was strictly for being peaceful. What's he going to have to say about this?"

"I don't know. Reckon I'll find out when I get back to the ranch."

"He's never had this happen to one of his people. Not as long as I've been around here, at least."

"I'll send the shirt back in a couple of days," I promised, reaching to my collar and giving it a jerk to pop the buttons down the length.

He brought the shirt back and helped me into it, although his attitude remained one of disapproval. As I turned to leave, he extended the glass, which he had replenished while going after the shirt.

"Take a slug of this," he ordered. "It'll help put a little bone back in your legs."

I hesitated, but he pushed the glass at me impatiently and I took it, downing a healthy gulp. It burned all the way down, and when it hit my stomach I thought it was going to come back up. He chuckled drunkenly at the face I made.

"I'll want to see that arm in about a week," he announced. "Sooner, if it starts to bother you or you think it's getting infected. You can bring the shirt back then."

"Thanks, Doc. How much do I owe you?"

He shook his head, grinning at me. "You've already paid. Some of them gold pieces slipped out of your pocket." He hoisted the glass, which he had taken back from me, staring at it with a mellow expression. "My supply of the nectar of the gods was running a bit low. Knew you wouldn't mind. You're all paid."

"Okay. Thanks again."

He cocked an eye at me leeringly as he offered a confidence. "'Course, I charged you a little extra to keep that other feller from chopping you up some more. Figured it might be worth it to you."

"Yeah," I said, and moved out into the night.

The street was dark as I pulled on my hat, which I had taken from the foot of the operating table. It seemed a little strange that I still had it after the intensity of the fight in the saloon. The street was massed with shadows except where a light appeared in a window here and there and in front of several business establishments, where torches on high poles threw off flickering, oil-fed illumination.

I retraced my steps along the street and turned a corner to look toward the Golden Dragon. My horse was still tied to the hitch rail in front of the place. As I approached, the sound of the same weary music came out into the stillness, backed by the low buzz of voices.

I moved close to the door, looking through the bead curtain at the group of seamen lined up at the bar. Others were gathered about the tables, conversations piling over one another in half a dozen languages, but there was no sign of either Slack or the girl.

I went back to the horse and mounted clumsily, reining the animal toward the wharfs. I had learned that morning, as I sought information, that one of the ships, a Danish tramp steamer, was due to sail that night, bound for the States after making several cargo stops in other Island ports. That was the ship I expected Slack to be on. It was supposed to sail at eleven, I recalled.

As I reached the pier, I pulled the horse into the shadow of a warehouse and sat watching as several seamen moved out on the dock, answered shouts from the deck, where a lantern burned in the night, then went up the gangplank in single file. One man was too drunk to make it and had to be helped by his companions.

As several more lanterns were lighted about the deck and orders were shouted harshly back and forth in what I supposed to be Danish, men began to rush about, making last-minute preparations for sailing. In the dim light I thought I recognized several of the drinkers from the Golden Dragon, but it was too dark for assurance.

Standing there in the darkness, running my hands along the ends of the reins uneasily while the horse nuzzled at my back, I began to worry that perhaps Slack had decided to stay and carry out his threat. The fears were interrupted, though, by the sound of steel-rimmed wheels on the coral-topped street, and I looked up to see a carriage halt at the head of the pier.

The driver got down and helped the girl to the ground. Between them, they aided the dark figure of Jeff Slack, whose face was swathed in bandages. He seemed uncertain, groping for the girl's arm for support as she turned and paid the driver. As the carriage drove away, she half led him along the pier to the gangplank.

I couldn't hear what was said, but one of the seamen came down the plank and helped Slack, half staggering, up to the deck, while the girl looked on. There was no parting gesture between them, no kiss of farewell. Slack didn't look back as he was led to the cabin and taken below.

Satisfied, I turned the horse and wearily headed back to the ranch.

Twelve

"What'd you do, kill him?"

Mark Hollman sat behind his desk, staring down at the double handful of gold coins I had thrown on the scarred wood.

"You told me to settle it," I growled. "There won't be any more cow stealing and he's left the Island. He won't be back."

"You still haven't told me who it was," the ranch manager said slowly, pushing the Chinese money into a pile, and looking up at me with a scowl. "And you haven't said what happened."

"Jeff Slack. I did some checking around the wharfs and found out he'd been selling butchered beef to ships taking on supplies in the harbor. When I went to see him, he admitted he was behind it. He had the money. I took it, put him on a ship and came back. As simple as that."

He was still frowning as he shook his head. "I told you I didn't want any trouble, Sam. This ranch has a good, solid reputation, and I'll not have it tainted."

"You told me not to take a gun, and you told me to stop the rustling. I believe that's a direct quote. I followed your orders on both counts. You have what's left of the money, and you ought to damned well be happy!"

My voice was impatient at his sudden turnabout. When he had told me to stop the thefts and butcherings, he hadn't been so cautious, but now that it was settled, the old instinct was back with him.

"How much trouble was there? You run afoul of the law at all?" he wanted to know, looking down at the gold.

"I doubt that they even knew Slack and I met. We held our little discussion in a spot that wouldn't look too kindly upon the law, I reckon. You won't hear anything from it."

"Slack? You hurt him at all?"

I lost my temper. "You're goddam right I hurt him. The bastard would've killed me if I'd give him the chance!" I leaned over the desk, spreading my arms to balance on the rough surface, staring into his face.

"And the next time you want a dirty job done, if you're going to try to tell me how to do it after it's done, don't bother. What I get as a foreman don't make that much difference!"

He reached out to lay a hand on my arm, the one with the bandage, and I winced. Alarm and suspicion came into his eyes as he looked at me, rising from the chair.

"Sorry, Sam. You're right about that, but I got something kind of special on my mind. You're right, like you said. When I told you to settle it, I meant it. I don't have a right to question how it was done, so long as no one got killed or bad hurt." His tone was dipped in the honey of apology as he came around the desk, but the expression was still in his eyes. It didn't change as his gaze went to my arm. I glanced down and saw that blood from the bandage had soaked through the shirtsleeve in a small, circular spot.

"What happened to your arm?" he asked sympathetically, reaching out as though to touch the stain. I pushed the hand away.

"Horse fell with me coming in this morning. I landed on a rock."

The look was still on his face and the frown came flooding back, as he stared at me, croaking, "I told you when you took this job that I expected the truth from my ramrod, Turk. I *want* it from you. *Now!*"

"Give me my time!" I grated at him. "I'm riding out. I'll be on the next boat out of Hilo!"

"What're you talking about?"

"You bastard, you know damned well what I'm saying. You ordered me to pull your chestnuts out of the fire. Now you're trying to slap my hands for it because I didn't let myself get burned. Is that plain enough?"

I was shouting at him without realizing it.

"Now wait, Sam. I don't want you to think I—"

"Dammit, Mark! You told me to run the outfit the way I thought best. That included getting rid of Slack. I didn't kill him and he ain't hurt too bad, and if it's the truth you're after, the sonuvabitch tried to carve me up like one of your sides of beef!"

"Listen to me, Sam!" He was almost pleading, yet not unbending enough that it could be classified that low.

"Figure my pay. I'll catch up a fresh horse and leave him in town."

"You mule-headed bastard," he declared, trying to hold his voice under control after regaining some of his composure. "I'm not figuring your pay, and you ain't riding out. Maybe you're right about my trying to stick too close to a line that none of us can see," he admitted slowly, "and I'll have to admit I said some things about getting rid of Slack while I was all heated up and wasn't thinking too straight."

"Better start thinking, then, before you start handing out them kind of orders," I said pointedly.

"You're staying on?"

I hesitated, staring at him thoughtfully. For a few moments I had been on top, saying the things I was thinking. The same thoughts I had had even back in Texas, when he had sold his small spread and drifted out of the country rather than get involved in the range war.

Now, though, I had lowered my defenses, and he knew he had me. He knew, without asking, that I wasn't going to leave. I did owe him something, I told myself. He had brought me here, even paying my passage from San Francisco, when I was running. He had given me a job and whatever small protection he could against my past.

Indirectly, I was thinking, he had been responsible for my being able to end my past. I hadn't been able to run away from that, though. I had had to send the past away from me, instead. That's what I was doing when Jeff Slack walked up that gangplank and boarded the Danish ship the night before.

"Yeah. I'm staying," I told him wearily. My arm suddenly bothered me, pain coursing up and down the nerves which had been slashed during the fight. "But maybe you'd better put into writing what my duties are supposed to be around here so we'll both know."

He smiled then, starting to grab my bad arm, then thought better of it. Instead, he put a hand on my other shoulder, gripping it heavily.

"No need for that," he declared. "Slack's gone and we won't need to worry about a thing like this coming up no more."

He turned back to the desk to pick up a letter, which he held close to his chest as he went on hurriedly.

"I told you a minute ago I needed you. We've got a lot of work to catch up on in the next while. A lot of it. Here. You'd better read this for yourself."

He pushed the letter toward me and turned to pick up his pipe from an ashtray and tamp down the partially burned contents with a thumb, while I looked down at the piece of stationery.

It bore the embossed monogram of the Palace Hotel in San Francisco and carried a date nearly two weeks previous. The writing was a bold scrawl in heavy, purple ink. Hollman touched a match to his pipe and blew a puff of smoke, watching me expectantly as I slowly read the contents:

My dear Mr. Hollman:

I know this epistle will serve as something of a surprise to you, but after all of these years of correspondence we finally are to meet in person.

My sister, Miss Rowena Fairson, and I are presently in the United States, having completed the first leg of an extended trip around the world. We have been lucky enough to arrange our schedule and passenger bookings so that we finally will be able to visit the ranch, which frankly is considered something of an inherited oddity by our family.

I will be the first to admit that I know nothing of this vocation called cattle ranching, but in my recent travels through this American West, I have seen numerous examples of how other cattle-raising enterprises are operated and shall look forward to seeing how our own operations may compare.

As it now stands, we are scheduled to arrive in Honolulu on February eighteenth, and we have been assured that we will have no difficulty in obtaining passage to your port of Hilo the following day. We assume that you will be on hand to meet us upon our arrival.

Needless to say, perhaps, we are looking forward to a most enlightening visit, and I am sincerely certain both my sister and myself will enjoy every moment of it.

Expectantly yours,
Richard H. Fairson

"How do you like that?" Hollman growled as I finished reading, folded the letter along the creases and handed it back to him. "He spends a month in the States, rides a train across a couple of ranges, and now he's all set to show us how to raise cattle at a profit!"

"You're borrowing trouble. The letter doesn't say anything like that."

He puffed angrily at the pipe, which had gone out, then turned to slam it into the ashtray in a show of frustration.

"It don't say it, but I can see it now. And his talk about past correspondence. The only person I've heard from since his old man died has been the family lawyer. Never heard from this lily-spined kid even once during all that time!" He began pacing the floor, hands clenched behind his back, glaring angrily at the floor. "Put in twenty of the best years of my life trying to make something out of this heap of lava, and he'll probably want to change everything I've done."

He halted and turned to glare at me. "I told you I needed you, and I meant just that. There's a lot of work we have to get done around here before they come. That gives us less than two weeks."

"We're short-handed now," I told him. "We won't be doing a helluva lot more without putting on some new people. What do you have in mind?"

"Lot of little things we've gotten behind on, Sam. Need a new roof on the bunkhouse. There's a lot of fence that needs fixing. That stretch between us and the Parkers especially. And I want to start cleaning out the herd again, getting rid of some more of that scrub stock. That new herd bull's supposed to be in this week, and there's no point in mixing up good blood with bad."

"It don't sound like much," I told him, "but it'll all take time."

"I'll send down to Hilo for some men to work around the ranch here," Hollman promised. "They can fix the roof and maybe put some new posts in that corral fence. Some of them are starting to rot off, it looks like."

"What about this bull?" I asked. "When's he due? What day?" Through stock buyers in San Francisco, Hollman had arranged for the Hereford bull, a purebred animal that had been advertised in one of the stock papers that came from the mainland on almost every ship. The price had been three thousand dollars, and there had been several months of correspondence between London and the ranch before the Fairsons' family lawyer had finally agreed to the expenditure.

With the money already spent, and additional shipping charges for getting the animal to the Islands, it was plain that Hollman was glad it was going to be on hand when the Fairsons arrived.

"They'll be unloading him off the *Star of Glasgow,*" he said. "That's next Thursday, ain't it?"

"Reckon it is," I nodded. "How do you figure to get that critter up here?"

"Drive him, I guess. Thought of loading him in a wagon, but he's too big for that. Besides, if he got out over the top or busted through the side, he might break a leg. I'll want you to handle getting him here."

"Too bad," I said with a grimace, and Hollman looked at me sharply.

"What's too bad?"

"Too bad Ben Low ain't here. I'd rather be in New York myself right now, with these people coming."

"Yeah," he growled. "Twenty years they let me sit here by myself before one of them finally wants to know what's going on. They ain't never been bashful about taking the money the place makes, though. Can't figure why they should get interested all of a sudden like this."

"I wouldn't worry, Mark," I offered soothingly. "If you ain't been feathering your own nest, you got nothing to worry about."

He looked up abruptly, glaring at me. "What kind of talk's that?"

"Relax. I joke."

He grinned, but he didn't enjoy it. He stepped forward to put a hand on my shoulder again.

"Sorry about the hassle a while ago, Sam. Probably did us both good, getting a chance to let off steam. And I'm glad you got rid of Slack without anyone getting hurt bad."

I nodded, wondering what his definition of *bad* might be if he ever heard the whole story.

"I'll get these people working," I told him. "There's a lot of fence to be built." I turned toward the door, but his voice stopped me.

"There's one thing more, Sam. Fire Martin!"

The order was unexpected, and it took me a moment to recover from my surprise.

"Why him?" I asked.

"No questions," he muttered, looking away uncomfortably. "Just get rid of him."

"I think we'd better go back to our earlier talk about me drawing my time. I thought we were agreed that I was running the crew. That the foreman would do the hiring and firing."

"I know," he agreed, still not looking at me, but picking up his pipe and concentrating on it again. "But this is a little different."

I turned back into the room to face him. "Look, Mark, I told you we're short now, and Drake's a good boy. Works hard. There's no reason for me to fire him, so I won't."

He glanced up at me, starting to speak, but I cut him off harshly. "After all this talk, we're right back where we started. You're trying to stick my hand into your fire to sort out the bad chestnuts. Just because the kid and Malia have been seeing a lot of each other ain't no reason for you to set yourself up as God. Someday she's going to want to get married, and there won't be much you can do to stop it."

I paused before I added on a new breath, "You don't know much about what goes on in your own daughter's head, Mark. She's scared of you!"

Surprise lighted his face for an instant, then was devoured by the heavier scowl. "There're some things maybe you don't know about this country, too, Sam. I told you once that the missionaries came here to do good and did well, but they weren't the only ones. Down in Hilo, when some of the first families get together, or even over in Honolulu, where they hold them society affairs, they tell the story about the beachcomber who drifted in without the price of a new pair of shoes, how he went to work and finally ended up marrying a member of the royal family."

He glanced at me to see how closely I was listening. It was becoming clear to me why Mark Hollman had always been so concerned about his own respectability and that of the ranch.

"From that time on, this bum did nothing but good. He made a good thing out of that marriage, if you can say that it ended up with him holding a good job and making money," he went on, with sarcasm veining his tones. "But them society people still don't look too kindly on him. He ain't invited to their fancy brawls. He's just an outsider who saw a good thing and took it! That man was me, Sam," he declared harshly. "And I ain't going to have my daughter marrying no saddle tramp and ending up in the same class! Get rid of him!"

"There's a lot of fence to be fixed," I replied levelly. "I'll put him out with a camp wagon and a couple of the boys. That should keep him away from the house here."

He still wanted to argue as I turned and stalked out the door, closing it behind me. As I stood listening at the panel for a moment, it seemed to me that I could hear heavy sobs of anger and frustration. But I couldn't be sure.

Thirteen

I didn't send Drake Martin away from the main ranch, as I had promised.

Instead, I put him to work with a paint brush, slapping a coat of whitewash on the time-weathered bunkhouse. In all the years since it had been built, this was the first protective coating it had seen, and the mixture soaked into the pores in the rough wood like water into a dry creek bed.

"Waste of time," Martin declared as he finished the front wall. "It'll look worse than if it wasn't painted at all. How you going to cover that up?"

"Give it a second coat," I told him quietly. He spat into the dust in front of the door and shrugged his disgust.

"I can think of a lot of things I'd rather be doing."

"Right now you're a painter," I told him bluntly. "Start slinging it! You got the house and corral to do when you're done here!"

He turned and put the brush on top of the pail, which was balanced on a step of the ladder, then turned slowly back to me, his face hard.

"Turk, are you riding me?" His words came slowly, measured between the force that each seemed to carry.

"You may be trying to run me off here the same as you did Slack, but it won't work," he went on, forcing a smile to his lips. "I'm staying!"

"Only if you follow orders."

"I'm following them. To the letter!" He turned and picked up the brush as I started away. Kimo, who had been painting at the other end of the structure, had been looking on, listening. He turned back to his work without speaking.

I stopped and turned back to Drake Martin. "What do you know about me running Slack off?"

"Malia told me," he said without looking around. "She told me what happened and what you did to him."

Slowly I walked back to him and stood looking at his back. "What else did she tell you?" If she had mentioned the day on the side of the volcano, it might explain his sullen attitude. "About me and Slack, I mean?"

He shrugged again. "That was it. Said he got mean with her, you heard it and run him off.

"I probably owe you some thanks," he went on tonelessly. "There'd of been trouble between him and me sure, if he'd been around much longer."

"Yeah. I know."

Joe Tam, an apron about his fat middle, had come out of the adjoining cook shack and was looking on with critical amusement.

"Whatsa mattah evahbody?" he wanted to know. "First time Kona rain come, alla white come off. Why make so pretty alla time now?"

I shook my head at him, grinning. "The boss man says so. He wants the place all beautied up when the big boss and his sister get here from England."

I didn't have to explain. I didn't know how many people Hollman had told about the expected arrival, but it had spread over the ranch like a locust plague and had been almost as popular.

Tam shook his head sourly. "Why they come?" he demanded. "We no need them here. All they mean's *pilikia*. Trouble for us. Don't like the way we run ranch, make changes."

He spread his hands in a motion of futility, turning to glare at the area of the structure where Kimo was lazily daubing whitewash.

"And alla that come off for sure, first Kona rain!"

He was probably right about the rains, I had to agree. What were termed "Kona rains" came on with the ferocity of a cyclone, the heavy winds beating the water before them. The force would be enough to chip the coating away in a matter of hours.

"I think Hollman can handle them," I told the Chinese cook. "Why should we bother about it? That's one of the things they pay him for."

Tam, his face still sour, shrugged in Oriental fashion and went back to his pots and pans.

Hollman and Himmler were in the office, stacks of ledgers and account books stacked before them. The bookkeeper was in shirtsleeves, and his eyes were red with lack of sleep as he glanced up at me. Then he nodded shortly and returned to his books.

No more than a dozen words had passed between us since the incident over the rifle and my short-lived suspicion that he was the sniper who had fired upon Malia and myself. I was certain that, in spite of our truce, there was a strange hatred deep within him, but he kept it well hidden. In fact, he seemed to be devoid of emotion. His single function in life seemed to be to add, subtract, multiply and divide with accuracy.

Hollman stood up, running his hands through his rumpled hair, scowling as he glanced at me, then back to one of the ledgers. "Well, you're the bookkeeper, so keep at it. The mistake has to be there somewhere. That much money just don't up and stampede away."

Himmler looked at him quickly, and for one brief instant there was an expression of pain and hurt behind his thick lenses. Then the wound was covered by the indifference of mechanical efficiency and he nodded.

"I was on it all night," he said quietly. "Maybe I'm just too tired to keep it straight."

"That's maybe it," Hollman agreed, putting a hand on the man's shoulder. "We've still got time before they show up. No point in trying to straighten it out all at once. You go ahead and get some sleep, then try it some more."

Himmler straightened, putting down his pencil in the crack of the book, allowing the suggestion of a smile to flicker across his lips. He reached for his black coat on the back of the chair and started to shrug into it.

"I could use some sleep."

He turned and started for the door, glancing at me again, and there was a questioning look in his eyes.

It was bad enough that he had been imprisoned by the Army for a shortage in his paymaster accounts and had admitted it to me. But it was worse that I should know there was a shortage now. And Hollman's comment about the money not being able to disappear by itself had added to it. He was scowling heavily as he shut the door behind him.

"What about that kid?" Hollman demanded. "I thought you were sending him up to the fence camp to help out."

"Not yet," I agreed. "I kept him around for a reason. I want him along to help bring that bull up tomorrow. I have a hunch that if he's any kind of an animal at all, he's going to be right unhappy after being cooped up on that ship all the way from the States. Drake does know how to handle stock, whether you approve of him or not."

"There're other men here that know as much as he does." Hollman was glaring at me, his hands clenched into fists.

"I thought we'd agreed that I was still the foreman. The job's supposed to cover handling the men."

"You're pushing it a little," he growled. "How many men you figure to need to move that bull?"

"Three. That way, I know the critter won't come to no harm and nobody'll get hurt."

"I'm going down tonight," he declared. "I'll help you bring him back."

I nodded agreement. "I'll see you at the hotel when we get in." I knew the name of the place where he always stayed when in Hilo on business.

"Check on the ship first," he ordered. "I may want to sleep late. No point in getting me up to sit around a wharf half the day."

"Sure."

"And get that kid up with that fence crew when we get back," he growled.

"Figured to. In fact, I'll have him pack his gear so he can pick it up when we get this far. Then we can take the bull on up to the high pasture with them prize heifers of yours."

"What's left of them." He was still thinking of the thirty head that Slack had turned into beef.

And his sullen attitude concerning Drake Martin undoubtedly had been brought about by the fact that two horses had been missing from the corral the evening before.

I had walked down in the moonlight to be certain there was water in the wooden tank and had found him leaning against the rail, counting them. It took only a glance to see that Drake's mount and the one Malia usually rode were missing. Whatever difficulty the two had experienced in the past had been patched up. They had been riding out alone nearly every evening. Drake often did not return until the rest of the crew was asleep and the light out.

It was nearly midnight last night when he came in, removing his boots at the door and creeping stealthily into his blankets.

"Why don't you tell him to stay away from her?" I suggested as Hollman turned away from the corral.

"You don't know her," he murmured. "If I did something like that, she'd make a point of seeing him. I'm afraid I spared the rod with that girl."

"She's your problem. Drake's mine," I told him, "but it's not my affair to meddle in his private life."

"And she figures it's not my place to meddle in hers," he admitted miserably. "Sometimes I start thinking how it might be if her mother was still alive to handle her. Then I realize that they'd probably stick together and tell me I'm all wrong."

"Maybe you are."

He didn't answer that. Instead, he turned to walk slowly toward the house, leaving me alone in the moonlight.

Drake Martin and I rode down to Hilo the following morning. I had stayed awake to talk to him when he came in late the night before. Again, he had been riding and the same two horses were gone from the corral.

I had told him that I wanted him to help with the bull and that, after that, he would be assigned to the fencing crew. He had listened to my instructions for him to pack his stuff so that he would be able to take it with him, then had nodded without comment, his face showing nothing.

He had touched a match to the coal-oil lamp and was busy at his bunk, making up a saddle roll and stuffing clothing into his saddle bags as I turned in. I had gone to sleep before he was finished.

Joe Tam had awakened us both before dawn, as I had instructed, and we had just finished a breakfast of ginger-spiced beef, eggs and fried rice, when the rest of the crew came staggering into the cook shack, some rubbing their eyes, others pulling on their clothing.

Briefly I outlined the day's work, putting Felipe, the Filipino rider, in charge, while Martin went out to saddle the horses. We were halfway to the coast before the sun came over the hills.

"This idea of putting me building fence your idea?" Martin asked sullenly, as he pulled up once to allow the horses to drink from a small spring.

"It's my idea. There's a lot to be done and they need

help." I kept my voice level as I stared at him. "Who'd you think it was?"

"Old Man Hollman, maybe."

Nothing more was said until we reached the wharf, where the *Star of Glasgow* was to tie up. There was no sign of the ship, and we found out from one of the workmen that it was not expected until noon.

"You're on your own till then," I told the younger man. "I'll leave a note at the hotel for Hollman, telling him the score. Be back here at noon and don't get drunk."

"I'll be here." Martin turned to mount his horse and rode away down the street without looking back. I asked a few more questions concerning the ship, then rode to the small, inexpensive hotel, where I left a note for Hollman.

The clerk said that he hadn't seen Mark all morning. His key was not on the hook behind the desk. He was keeping his promise to sleep late, probably nursing a hangover, I decided. It was a little before nine and, as I walked out into the bright sunlight, I wondered how I would fill the time before the ship arrived.

My arm was healing nicely and Joe Tam had rebandaged it for me twice, asking no questions as to how I had received the long gashes. I decided, though, to let the doctor look at it. As I led my horse down the street toward his office, I noticed the half-naked children playing in the street. It was some kind of game. All were armed with spears and clubs made from bits of native wood and seemed to be wrestling on an embankment between two of the high buildings. Suddenly, one side of the mock armies seemed to capitulate and were hurled over the embankment, rolling down to the undergrowth below, while the victors shouted native cries of conquest.

The children were re-enacting the victory battle of King Kamehameha, I realized, hearing the name mentioned several times among the rattle of Polynesian dialects.

Kamehameha, the king who had welded the Hawaiian

Islands together into an empire, reached greatness on the island of Oahu, when he backed his enemy to the edge of a cliff called the Nuuanu Pali, and forced those who refused to surrender over the edge, where they crashed to their death a thousand feet below.

As I walked on, the vanquished were returning to the edge of the street, demanding that the tables be turned and they be allowed the role of the victorious army. The argument was close to blows as I tied my horse before the doctor's office.

The gray, weary woman led me into the office and began to strip the bandage off my arm. A few moments later, the doctor appeared. He was drunk, staring at me from the doorway leading to the rear of the house in a wise, owlish manner, reaching up to adjust his glasses with the hand that didn't hold the drink.

"Well, well," he muttered thickly, "if it isn't our cowboy gladiator. I trust the arm hasn't fallen off."

He came into the room and stood weaving back and forth as he bent to inspect the wound, reaching out to grasp the end of one of the catgut stitches and pull at it speculatively. I winced under the sting of pain, and he laughed.

"You heal quickly, sir," he declared grandly. "It is time to take them out." He motioned to his wife, and she went to the instrument case and returned with a pair of small scissors and tweezers. The surgeon took another sip from the glass and handed it to her as he took the instruments and bent close to me, raising my arm and placing it on the operating table, which was next to my chair.

All signs of his drunken state were gone as he carefully cut the stitches and pulled them smoothly from the small blue-edged holes, dropping each into a metal tray which his wife had put beside him. The lean fingers worked deftly until he was done and had swabbed the arm with iodine.

"Leave it open," he ordered thickly, breathing Scotch fumes in my face. "It will heal quickly now."

He straightened to smile at me as I reached for my wallet. He waved his hand airily. "No payment," he declared. "This is my gift to the Hawaiian Islands. And this"—he lifted the nearly empty glass to look at it, his face twisted into a mask of bitterness—"is its gift to me!"

He downed the rest of the drink and turned to hand the glass to his wife. "Get me another," he muttered with a weariness that matched hers. "And get one for our customer, too. Alcohol is an excellent curative. It can cure all the ills and troubles of mankind for a time.

"A very short time," he added.

The woman hesitated, as though about to speak, then turned to disappear into the back room, closing the door behind her.

"I am returning to civilization, my good man," the surgeon announced. "I have had enough of putting up with witchcraft and matching talents with a native priest. We are returning to Boston, where I can at least drink myself to death like a gentleman!"

"No business?" I asked.

"No business," he agreed with a vague wave that encompassed the island, the world, the universe in general. "These heathens may someday learn the advantages of modern medicine, but not so long as they think there is a devil god hidden in every stone and white men want to keep them thinking that for personal gain.

"Yes," he went on dreamily, "today I have made my decision. I shall return to Boston. The decision was made after many other decisions, you understand. A night of decisions! I lined up every bottle in the house and spent the night making decisions as to which one to drink from next."

"Leonard! Stop it!" The woman was standing in the doorway, staring at him with the frustration of one who has been hurt and who doesn't know how to strike back. The doctor turned to look at her.

"And it was my wife who helped with the decision of

decisions," he said quietly and with a precision that hid his drunken speech for an instant. "Each time I took a drink, she told me we should go back to Boston. 'This is no place for a man of your talent,' she kept telling me. And she was right. It is no place."

He lowered his head and sagged against the operating table. The woman came forward and handed me one of the tumblers, starting to set the other aside. He straightened abruptly and took it from her, gulping it down.

"No place for talent," he murmured tiredly as he lowered the glass to look at it. "But there is no place for talent anywhere."

I watched as he pulled himself erect and walked out of the room to refill the glass. His wife followed, hovering behind him like a mother brood hen.

I drank the Scotch down quickly, left the glass on the table and went out into the street, down to the dock.

Fourteen

That afternoon the ship arrived with the bull. The animal, after being dropped over the side of the ship in a sling, nearly escaped before I was able to loop a lariat through the ring in his nose and the other two had each got a rope around his neck.

Hollman took the lead, inducing the animal through the streets by the lead ring, while Martin and I rode on the flanks, ropes looped about our saddle horns with little slack. In this way, we had the animal in a triangle. If he made a lunge for one of us, the man on the other flank held him in tow. If he tried for Hollman's mount, we both were there to discourage him with the nooses about his neck.

The parade through Hilo had created quite a stir, and men, women and children of half a dozen nationalities lined the street leading up from the wharf to admire the new bull and to offer laughing comments on our means of control.

One youngster had dodged in behind Hollman's animal, setting himself up as a laughing target. The bull had lunged at the child, and the boy had dodged out of the animal's path, while the crowd roared approval at the show of daring. Mark's aim was better than the bull's as he stung the surprised hero across the buttocks with a rope end, cursing him soundly.

Martin had been drinking and sat slack in his saddle, watching the animal sullenly throughout the trip, his eyes never leaving the broad, red-colored back. It had been a slow trip and wearing, as the bull spent the first half trying to gore a horse, and the second half fighting the ropes as weariness wore him down. We finally reached the ranch without any serious trouble.

"Come in the house for a minute while Martin gets his gear," Hollman ordered as we reached the ranch yard. "I'm going to let the two of you take him on up to the high pasture by yourselves."

I had just finished tying the bull to the corral fence and had swung down, facing the ranch manager. Drake Martin was already on his way to the bunkhouse, leading his horse.

I nodded and turned to follow Hollman, who walked with a stiff back, head high. He hadn't said over a dozen words all the way up the trail, even when the bull became difficult.

"We might do better to keep that bull here tonight," I suggested. "He's pretty tired to take on up."

"I want him up there. And I want Martin up there, too," Hollman growled, eying me as he turned before the house.

He turned on his heel and stalked away, disappearing into the house. As I started back to the corral, the thought was with me that this situation over Malia was getting out of hand.

It was growing dark as we forced the heaving bull up the last portion of rocky trail to the meadow bordering the volcano and I slipped from my horse, looking toward Drake Martin.

"I'm going to take the line off that nose ring," I told him. "Keep your rope tight till I get it done."

He nodded, slumping easily in his saddle. I followed down the rope I held until I reached the bull's head. He stood with legs spread wide, blowing at the high grass. As I raised his head, I could feel the sweat beneath the heavy hair.

"Probably lost a couple of hundred pounds," I ventured,

untying the knot in the ring. The bull's nose was bleeding where the ring had pulled at the tender flesh.

As I dropped the rope and began to coil the lariat, the rope about the animal's neck suddenly went slack and the animal dived at me with a bawl of anger. I threw myself aside, falling, and landed on my bad arm.

"Goddamit, I said keep that rope tight!" I snarled at Martin as I rolled up to my knees. The bull tried to bolt, hit the end of the rope and was swung about as Martin's horse grunted under the unexpected tug against the saddle girth. The bull came toward me again, head lowered, horns set for a hook.

I slammed the braided rope end across the animal's nose, and he bawled with rage. As he went past, I grabbed him and dug in my heels. One hand went to the nose ring, the other went across the top of his head to grab the tip of the horn. As I twisted it up and away from me, the animal fell. The wind went out of me as a part of his weight crashed down on top of me.

"Get this rope off him so I can let him up," I shouted at Drake. He was already off his horse, sprinting toward me. The animal struggled to rise, bawling in anger and fright. Quickly Martin stripped off the rope and stood looking at me uncertainly.

"Get on your horse," I ordered. "He's going to be mad as hell when he gets on his feet."

Martin mounted, grabbed the reins of my horse and turned him about for a fast mount. By nudging the bull, I released the weight on my leg as he struggled in response. Still holding him, I got on my feet, bending over him. Before the freed animal could stagger to his feet, shaking his head, I was in the saddle, riding away, Martin beside me.

The bull stared after us for a moment, then turned and saw the herd of young heifers. With new thoughts, he trotted toward them.

"You're in charge of that fence job," I told the younger

man as we pulled up, turning our horses to look after the disgruntled animal. "See that those clowns keep working."

"Sorry about letting that rope slip," he said slowly, rolling a cigarette. "Might have got you killed."

"Yeah. You just might have done that."

He looked up, puzzled at my tone, then returned his eyes to his cigarette. "Heard some talk," he said thoughtfully. "Was at a place called the Golden Dragon this morning. Heard that Jeff Slack has left town for keeps. Heard he ain't quite the same man."

"I heard he'd left, too," I agreed cautiously, wondering what he was leading up to.

"You don't suppose being sent up here to string wire is the first step in my leaving, too, do you?" he asked, his voice still quiet. Too quiet. There was no expression on his face to tell his real thoughts behind the question.

"Not that I know of. You're up here because you're needed."

"Seems to me Hollman's in a hellish hurry to get some fence built before that Englishman shows up. If I leave, though, it won't be the same way Jeff Slack did, Mister Turk." There was warning in his tone, but he seemed to be concentrating on lighting the cigarette.

"You can still make it up to the camp before they're done with chow, if you hurry," I told him.

"Yeah. I reckon I can, at that." He flicked the match away, lifted a hand in mocking salute and spurred his horse away at a fast trot. He didn't look back as he cut toward the end of the bench in the direction of the line between the Fairson and Parker interests.

I turned my horse and started down the trail from the pasture. At the foot of the bench the horse stumbled with weariness, and I turned across the open ground toward a clump of trees hidden in a depression a few hundred yards away.

A horse suddenly whinnied, and my own animal returned

the greeting as I pulled him up cautiously. At a slow walk I rode toward the trees, wondering about the sound. None of our horses were grazed on this part of the range, I knew, but it could be a stray animal that had sought out the water I knew was there.

As I rode into the trees, I saw Malia's mount tied there. She came out of the brush and looked up in surprise at the sound of my own animal. She carried a wet sarong over one arm, and was buttoning her shirt with the other.

"What're you doing here?" Her voice sounded like she was accusing me of walking into her bedroom in the middle of the night.

"My horse is beat. He needs a drink." I swung down and led the animal to the broad, black pool. He nuzzled the water, snorting with expectancy, then plunged his nose into it, sucking noisily.

It was a beautiful spot. Flowers floated on the surface at the far end of the pool, while a formation of lava rose above it. From somewhere above, a fine stream tumbled over the rock, throwing up a spray as it struck the water. I had seen the trees before and knew they meant water, but I had never bothered to investigate.

"I came here to swim," the girl said behind me. "I was just leaving."

"Good. I'll ride back with you." As I turned, she was already mounting. I led my own horse out of the trees before getting into the saddle.

"Nice spot," I ventured.

"I've been coming here since I was a child," she told me. "No one else ever does."

Her horse whinnied again, and she stiffened, frowning as we turned toward the ranch headquarters. Somewhere up on the bench trail another horse answered.

I glanced over my shoulder and, in the dusk, thought I made out a horse, but couldn't be sure. But I was certain someone else had been at the pool. The hoof tracks in the mud at the water's edge were larger than those of her own mount. Drake Martin's horse would just about fit into them, I decided. He probably had doubled back on the trail after leaving me, planning to meet her there again.

There was something else I wasn't sure of, though. I couldn't help wondering whether Drake's carelessness in allowing the rope to slip on that bull had really been accidental!

Fifteen

Hollman's welcome for Richard and Rowena Fairson was a great success. He had rented a carriage rather than use the spring wagon to transport them to the ranch, after meeting them at the ship.

Malia and I had ridden down with him, while he drove the carriage, the seat beside him loaded with orchid and ginger leis. His daughter and the old Japanese woman had made them up late the night before, wrapping them in damp paper so they would not wilt on the trip down to Hilo.

Malia and I waited at the carriage, while Hollman went looking for the arrivals amid the laughing, shouting group of people and their relatives who had arrived from Honolulu aboard the small interisland steamer. The Fairsons were not hard to find, for most of the passengers were native. They stood amid the melee, looking about uncomfortably until Mark pushed through the mob to reach them.

Fairson was a tall, athletic type in his early thirties, wearing a formal expression and a tweed suit. His carefully blocked hat had been knocked askew in the mob, and he took it off to straighten it as Malia moved in on him, threw one of the orchid leis about his neck and kissed him soundly.

"I say, miss," he muttered in surprise, drawing back. The hand that held the hat dropped. So did the hat. I handed the necklaces of flowers I was holding to Hollman and stopped to retrieve the expensive beaver.

Mark advanced on Rowena Fairson, one of the leis spread to put about her head, but she retreated, holding up a hand, eying him with doubt.

"Just an old Island custom," he told her soothingly. "No harm meant."

Malia was giggling, while Fairson was still trying to regain his composure, eying her speculatively. Rowena paused to glance toward her with a frown, and Hollman closed in, throwing the lei about her neck and planting a kiss on her cheek. She stiffened, glaring around at us.

"What a disgusting custom," she said coldly.

"Oh, now, I wouldn't say that." Her brother was staring at Malia with a bold smile. "I found it rather delightful."

"She's right on one point," the girl said bluntly. "It's a custom. Nothing more." Fairson took the hint and turned to Hollman, extending his hand.

"You must be Mark Hollman. I'd have known you anywhere."

Rowena shook hands with him, a curtain of reserve still between them, and Malia and I were introduced. Rowena was nearly as tall as her brother and spoke in a clipped, sharp voice, every word seeming to have a value with her. She could have been pretty, but seemed to have made a deliberate effort to avoid the appearance. Her only concession was a gown in the latest San Francisco fashion and the flower-bedecked hat that was perched precisely on her head.

The buggy was a tight squeeze, with Malia driving, Fairson in the middle and his sister on the other side, but Fairson seemed to enjoy it and carried on a running account of their travels since leaving London, while Hollman and I rode flank on each side of the bouncing vehicle.

Another *luau* had been planned for the evening, and it went off with great success. Fairson took readily to the *okolehao* that Mark kept pushing before him and would have engaged in one of the hula dances with the women if his sister hadn't discouraged it coldly.

"I say," he declared with a silly grin, "this is even better than that circus we saw in St. Louis. The Barnum and Bailey affair."

His sister nodded agreement, but that was all. She seemed devoid of all emotion, watching the progress of the party with disinterest except to lift a cup of the whiskey to her lips occasionally and sip at it.

I had expected Malia to perform her Tahitian dance, but she wasn't even present. When I asked Hollman about her, he told me that she wasn't feeling well and had decided to stay in her room. I noticed also that the fence crew had not been invited to the affair.

I would have been willing to bet a month's pay that her horse was missing from the corral and that Drake Martin was absent from the camp. The only person who might have been interested in such a bet, though, would have been Hollman. Winning from him after recent events would have been poor judgment. Besides, it was none of my affair, even if he had attempted to make it so by having me send Martin to the most distant area of the ranch.

Kimo had been given the job of keeping the guest's bamboo cups full and circled the circle of laughing, shouting people, ignoring the dancers with a whiskey-filled gourd in his hands. He halted to fill my cup, but I shook my head at him, and he moved on to the Fairsons.

As he turned to Rowena, his foot caught on Fairson's highly polished, fashionable shoe and he went catapulting down into her lap, the gourd beneath him.

There was a scream from Rowena's thin, prim lips that would have done credit to a raped tiger. It wasn't an expression of fear nor surprise, but a cry of outraged anger.

Kimo rolled up to his knees, mouthing embarrassed apologies in Polynesian syllables, not realizing that all that remained in his extended hand was the broken neck of the container. Its contents and broken fragments of gourd rested in a dark, receding puddle in the Englishwoman's ample lap.

"You stupid little heathen!" she screamed and slapped the boy sharply across the face. Surprise and hurt leaped into his eyes as a hand went up to the red imprint and his mouth fell open slackly. Hurriedly, he pulled himself away from her, cringing while his eyes became accusing and unforgiving.

"Rowena! What's the matter with you?" her brother snarled at her. "He's only a child! He didn't mean to do it!"

"Look at my dress! It's ruined! Do you hear me? Ruined!" The woman was almost in tears, and I realized suddenly that she was drunk. Very drunk. The music had stopped and there was a dead silence.

"It's all your fault!" she raged at her brother. "I didn't want to come on this awful, boring trip, but you had to drag me along!"

"It was for your own good, Rowena. I tried to explain that to you." Fairson had moved closer to her, looking into her face with protective, brotherly tenderness. As he tried to put an arm about her shoulders, she pushed it away and rose rapidly to her feet, staggering off into the darkness.

Hollman had been looking on dumbly, as had all of the Hawaiians gathered about the torchlit circle. Suddenly he started to his feet and Fairson also rose, his face red with alcohol and shame.

"Never mind," he muttered to Mark. "I'll talk to her. I'll take care of her."

"Take care of her, hell!" Hollman snarled. "She owes that boy an apology, and I mean to see that she gives it!"

Formality took over as the Englishman stiffened, his head going back. "Now see here, sir," he said sternly. "I will admit that an apology is necessary, and I extend it for her." His eyes flicked down to Kimo, who was still on his knees.

"I'm sorry, young man. Most sorry, indeed. My sister didn't mean it, really. She has been quite ill. It is my fault more than hers, I fear.

"Perhaps I shouldn't have brought her away from home,"

he said to Hollman softly, as though guarding a family skele-
ton from the others. "She hasn't been quite herself for several months. An unhappy love affair, you know. Been drinking quite heavily, too." He hesitated uncertainly, as though
feeling there was something more that should be said, but
not knowing what it should be. "I really must look after her."

He turned and moved into the darkness toward the house,
Hollman looking after him. Slowly the ranch manager
turned back to the others and forced a grin. "Go ahead," he
said wearily. "Have fun. It's nothing to worry about."

Someone struck a chord on a guitar and a buzz of voices
began, but it wasn't the same. The fun was gone and there
was a blanket of uncertainty hanging over the group as
husbands and wives, even some of the children, exchanged
wondering glances. Most didn't know what had caused the
diversion, but whatever it was, they hadn't liked it. Especially Kimo's being slapped. There was sullen displeasure in
some of the low mutterings in the background. Even the
music had lost some of its flavor, sounding low and ominous
as the musicians frowned over their instruments. The torches
had burned low, allowing deep shadows to hang over the
group.

Hollman sat down beside me and reached for his cup,
gulping down the raw native drink and making a wry face,
trying to ignore me.

"I'm sorry, Mister Hollman," Kimo said slowly. "I meant
to make no trouble." He had risen and was looking down at
the ranchman.

"It wasn't your fault, boy," he returned thickly. "Don't
worry no more about it."

The boy nodded and turned away. Hollman glanced at
me scowling.

"I didn't think you had it in you, Mark, rising up on your
back legs that way. Ain't exactly in keeping with your live-
and-let-live policy." The scowl he offered dared me to say
something. The "something" was the right thing apparently.

"That bitch'll probably have her brother fire me for that," he declared bitterly, "but she ain't talking to none of my people like that. Not as long as I'm running this rat race!"

"She'll be sorry about it when she sobers up," I promised. "She may be too proud to come around and apologize, but I have a hunch she'll talk her brother into leaving here a lot faster than they figured on doing. The great lady won't want to face these people any longer than she has to, once she wakes up and remembers what happened."

"I hope so," he said gloomily, "but she nor nobody else is going to slap that boy around." He reached for another gourd nearby, filled his cup and reached out to raise the level of mine.

"Think of something to drink to," he ordered wearily. "On second thought, let's just drink to drinking."

As he raised the bamboo section, there was a far-off look in his eyes, and I wondered if he had checked the corral and found his daughter's horse missing. Or whether he was just tired of fighting for respectability. Whether he had begun to realize that respectability isn't born of knowing the right people, but of learning not to run away from yourself.

I chuckled suddenly and he turned to me, glowering.

"What's so damned funny?" he wanted to know.

"Nothing. Just remembering something that happened to me once. I was just a kid when I poured a drink in the lap of a dance-hall gal. The swinging door of that saloon got torn clear off, she threw me out so hard."

He chuckled, too, but there was no humor in it. And that wasn't what I had been thinking of. The comparison between Hollman and me had suddenly struck me. I had always looked down on him for running out on the range war back in Texas. Yet, hadn't I done the same thing when the going had got rough and someone was after me? There really wasn't much difference.

As we sat there talking, the music stopped and the Islanders began to rise, drifting toward us in small groups.

Hollman saw them and stood up, weaving back and forth unsteadily. For once, he had forgotten his rule to fake his drinking for the benefit of the *paniolos*.

As they passed, bidding him goodnight and saying how much they had enjoyed the *luau*, he stood nodding and mumbling answers to them. Joe Tam and Kimo began to clear away the cluttered remains of the native feast in the dimming torchlight.

"Well, I reckon I'd better get some sleep," Hollman muttered. "Fairson says he wants to see the ranch in the morning. I'll be spending a lot more time in a saddle than I'm used to."

He started to turn, but halted at the sound of a running horse. The animal seemed to pull up near the corral, then was spurred on toward us, the rider having seen the light from the torches. It was Akuna Kumakelani, one of the riders from the fence camp.

He swung down from his horse and came running into the light, pausing to look around in surprise at finding the people gone, then spotted Hollman and myself. He came toward us, a worried frown twisting his dark features.

"Big *pilikia*, boss," he gasped. "You no like ver' much."

"What is it, Akuna?" I asked him quickly.

"Why ain't you up at that fence camp?" Hollman wanted to know.

"Somebody killed the bull. I think you want to know," he bleated.

Hollman seemed stunned for a moment as I clamped a hand on the rider's shoulder. "The one that just came in from the States?"

He nodded vigorously. "We hear gun up in pasture. Go up to look. Somebody shoot him right in eye."

The drunkenness was fading out of Hollman's face, forced out by shock, as I jerked my head toward the Hawaiian's horse.

"Turn your horse in the corral and sleep in the bunkhouse tonight. Too late for you to ride back," I told him.

Kumakelani stood looking from one to the other of us for an instant uncertainly, then turned away slowly to take up the reins. Tam, who had been too far away to overhear the news, came up, holding a gourd and shaking it near his ear with a wide grin.

"Fine *luau*, boss. Everybody like. Drink all the whiskey but this little bit. Here."

He extended it toward Hollman, who took it, turned the container upside down and watched the whiskey trickle out, soaking into the black sand. Tam was staring at him in confusion.

"Somethin' bad, boss? No like *luau? Kau kau* no good?"

"It was a good brawl, Joe. Real great," Mark Hollman ground out bitterly. "A real success."

He turned and broke the gourd across the trunk of a palm tree with a vicious, frustrated snarl.

Sixteen

I had been right on one point. The Fairsons had agreed by morning that they had seen enough of the ranch and that it was time they should be moving on.

"My sister is rather eager to visit some relatives in Australia," Fairson lied with magnificence. "There is a ship bound for there from Honolulu in two or three days."

"I hope she's feeling better," Mark Hollman sympathized, also lying. "But you'll want to go over the books with us, of course. You'll want to know what kind of shape the ranch is in."

"I've had a complete accounting each quarter from my representatives in London," the Englishman declared. "I am quite satisfied with the way the ranch is being operated, Mister Hollman."

"I'm glad to hear that," Mark told him, "but I wouldn't feel quite right if you left without going over the books some. Besides, we've had a little bad luck lately."

Fairson suddenly was interested, allowing a brow to rise with curiosity. "Bad luck? How is that?"

"A rustler slaughtered thirty head of our best two-year-old heifers," Hollman told him slowly. "Sold the meat in Hilo to some of the outbound ships. We put a stop to that, though."

"As long as it's ended, then, there wouldn't seem to be much more that can be done about it. No point in worrying about it now, is there?"

"That ain't all of it, though, Mister Fairson. Word came down last night after you'd left the *luau* that someone shot that bull we just paid three thousand dollars for."

"Good Lord," the Englishman gasped. "They told me the Wild West was tamed. Hasn't that influence reached this far?"

Hollman shook his head, eying the owner sternly. "I don't know what brought this on, Mister Fairson. It's the first time anything like this has happened in all the years I've been here." He nodded toward me. "Turk's going up there this morning to see what he can find, but it's been raining up in the mountains. He probably won't find much. Tracks of whoever did it'll be washed out."

"Perhaps I should look over the books with you," Fairson decided with slow-worded meaning. "I trust that my sister and I can still be taken back to Hilo before night to make arrangements for passage?"

"Sure. I want to do some checking on the range myself this afternoon, but we'll have someone drive you down."

"I probably won't see you again, if you're leaving that soon, sir," I told the Englishman, and we shook hands. I walked out of the office as Himmler opened one of the thick ledgers and began to explain to him the business details of the enterprise, Hollman looking over the bookkeeper's other shoulder.

Akuna Kumakelani was waiting for me in front of the ranch house, his own horse and mine saddled and ready. I had told him in the bunkhouse that morning that I would ride back to the high pasture with him to investigate the dead bull.

As we mounted and rode out between the corral and the bunkhouse, he looked glumly to where some of the other men were saddling mounts.

"Payday," he grunted. "Everybody else go to town, get drunk, take girls. We sit up there, build more fence."

"You'll get a couple of days off when it's done," I promised.

"How're you and the rest of the boys getting along with the *haole?*"

"Drake Martin?" He shrugged noncommittally. "He tells us what to do. We do it. He listens to bird calls."

"What? What're you talking about?"

He turned in his saddle to grin at me slyly. "Sometimes he hear bird call over the ridge. Right away, he saddle up to go and look at it. Sometimes don't come back for hours. Sometimes at night, too. Funny. Don't know about any night birds."

"How about female night birds? Know any of them that talk at night?"

"Not that ride horses," he declared, his grin widening. "Every time we hear bird at night, then another horse leave with his."

"How about last night? You hear a bird?"

He frowned with pretended thought, then shook his head. "No. No bird, but maybe Martin, he hear one. Ride away just after dark. Come back about morning."

I didn't have to ask anymore. Malia's horse had been gone from the corral. I had noticed that fact after the *luau* had broken up and Hollman had staggered off toward the house. The girl and Martin were continuing their nightly meetings. The bird call probably was her way of letting him know she had arrived.

"Martin ever say anything? He sore about being sent up there with the rest of you?"

The Hawaiian shrugged again, keeping his eyes on the trail. "He funny feller. Not talk much at all. At night we sing, play ukulele. He just sit and stare at the sky. Not a happy man. Never say anything about anything much."

"You heard the shot and went out to look? That's when you found the bull?"

The *paniolo* nodded glumly.

"Was Martin still in camp then?"

"Yeah. Still there. Gone when we come back, though. I start down to ranch to tell you then."

"You didn't see Martin on the way down, huh?"

He offered that same shrug. "Dark. Ride fast. See nothing."

I felt a sensation of slow relief spread through me. Ever since he had come with the word of the dead animal, the thought had been clinging to the back of my mind that Martin might have fired the shot. It would have been childish, I realized, but it could have been his way of getting even with Hollman for sending him away from the ranch. In spite of my telling him that his banishment to the fence camp had been my idea, I was sure he had blamed Malia's father.

As we neared the tree-surrounded pool, where I had discovered Malia a few days earlier, I pulled up and told Akuna that I wanted to check some water holes and for him to go on back to the fence camp. He nodded without speaking, then rode away. He had told me earlier where I could find the carcass of the animal.

I rode into the trees, dismounted and walked down to the water's edge. There had been several heavy rains since I was here the first time, and the tracks had been washed away. But there were fresh imprints. Those of small, bare feet and a pair of high-heeled boots. It was plain that Martin and the girl had been using this as a meeting place when he could steal away from the job.

It wasn't hard to spot the dead bull. The rest of the herd was gathered about the fallen sire curiously, some approaching close enough to nuzzle the red hair, then drawing back at the smell of death. The cows turned to look toward me with mournful eyes as I rode up and dismounted. They scattered slowly as I walked over to the animal and looked down at it.

It had been a good shot. Intentional. The animal had been shot through the left eye, the bullet channeling downward and coming out its neck. The hole was clean where the bullet had come out, testifying that a rifle had been used. A pistol bullet probably would have lodged somewhere inside the animal's head. If it had come out, there would have been a larger hole. The downward angle showed that the animal had been shot from the back of a horse. The eyeball had been shattered by the force of the bullet, but I was sure it had been fired from a .30-30 carbine!

Involuntarily, I straightened, flinching against the bullet I expected to feel between my back ribs, but there was nothing more than the soft lowing of one of the heifers and the call of a bird. My horse was contentedly cropping the graze a short way off.

There were tracks, but I didn't follow them. They led away toward the trail that twisted back and forth up the side of the volcano. There would be no way of following them there. Even steel shoes would leave little, if any, trail. Besides, whoever had shot the animal would be a long way off, I told myself.

Rather than leave the carcass lying there to rot, I looped my lariat about the hind legs and dragged it toward the face of the volcano, finally maneuvering it beneath a ledge. Leading the horse out of the way, I climbed up the face of the cliff until I found a large boulder, which I sent crashing downward. The debris and bits of rock and lava which followed made an adequate grave marker even for three thousand dollars worth of purebred beef.

"First time I was ever sorry not to have buzzards around," I told the horse as I mounted and started back across the bench to the trail leading downward.

Burying the carcass took longer than I thought. It was midafternoon by the time I hit level ground at the bottom of the trail and spurred toward the ranch headquarters. The grove shading the spring-fed pool was beginning to appear dark in its own shadows as it loomed in the depression at my flank.

The horse smelled the water and started to toss his head, trying to swing toward it, but I drove the spurs into his side and he leaped forward. At that moment a shrill scream tore away the veil of quiet.

I pulled the horse into a rear, as there was another scream. The terrorized cry was coming from the pool. As the animal's front hooves dug into the dirt, I swung him toward the closely spaced trees, kicking viciously at his flanks. The scream was repeated as I hit the edge of the grove and pulled up the mount, leaving its back before it had come to a full stop.

"Don't! You can't! They'll kill you!" It was Malia, her voice filled with fear, half pleading, half threatening. I ran along the open path leading to the water, and halted as I saw the twisted, scarred face.

The wet sarong which clung to her figure was partially torn away, and her hair was heavy with dirt as the girl struggled on the sloping embankment leading down to the water. Jeff Slack, eyes afire with desire, his lips made even more cruel in their tight, wolf smile by the blue-edged, half-healed scar running down from his mouth, was muttering savagely, "You've been rolling those eyes at everything in pants! It's about time you paid attention to me!"

"Don't touch me! I'll kill you myself!" The girl was screaming the words at him as he reached up to tear away the flowered print, laughing at her cruelly.

"Call Turk on me, will you? He ain't around now to protect you. You might as well give up and enjoy it!"

The girl screamed again and he slapped her across the cheek, the mud on his hand leaving a dark print. As the girl's head was jerked to one side under the blow, she saw me and stiffened beneath him, her struggles ceasing.

"Help me!" she pleaded softly, looking over his shoulder at me. Slack stiffened, realizing someone was behind him, and he turned, recognition lighting his inflamed eyes. He tried to roll away from the girl as I dived toward him, my body straightening into a flat arrow of weight.

My shoulder struck him in the chest, and he grunted his

surprise as we went over and over in the soft dirt. His hands were clawing at my face, his thumbs seeking my eyes as I tried to pound fists into his chin and nose.

His knee came up to catch me in the groin, and a thousand red stars shot through my brain. Weakness seemed to capture my muscles as sickness welled up in my stomach, the taste of bile strong in my mouth. I spat it into his face as I heard the girl scream again, the sound muffled in my own pain.

Suddenly Jeff Slack drove a fist into my neck and rolled free. I grabbed for him, but a foot caught me in the chest, sending me over on my back. Blackness clogged my sight as I struggled to my knees and heard a sharp gasp from the girl somewhere behind me.

"Don't move!" Slack's voice rasped heavily. "You and me got some business to finish just as soon as Mister Turk leaves us."

He was standing there grinning at me, a six gun in his hand. For the first time I noticed the worn holster buckled about his waist, the tip tied down by a strip of latigo about his right leg.

"You're going to leave us, Turk, for keeps!" he declared slowly, savoring the taste of the sentence. That's what it was. A death sentence.

I tried to speak, but my stomach twisted in pain, and I was on my hands and knees, vomiting as his words came over the retching sound.

"That's the way I figured you'd be, Turk. Big gun from Texas!" His voice was filled with amused sarcasm. "Big man with his face in the dirt, heaving up his guts! You're scared. Look at me and tell me you're scared!"

His feet came into view and, still sick, I grabbed for one of them. My reward was a flash of pain across the back of the head as the gun barrel tore at my scalp.

"That's it, Turk! Be brave. Be brave on your knees, if you want."

He had stepped back, and the sound of the hammer being thumbed back was the sound of doom. Malia was standing there with nothing to cover her nakedness, head lowered, shoulders heaving with the measure of her shocked hysteria.

"You didn't really think I'd leave without getting a chance at you, did you?" Slack wanted to know. "And a chance at the girl, like you had that day I took the shots at you up on the mountain? All I did was take that ship around to Kona and get off. I've been around ever since, waiting for you."

"You shot the bull, then."

"Sure. I figured that'd hurt Hollman in the pocketbook. That's where he seems to hurt worst, even if it ain't *his* money." Mockery was heavy in his tone as he went on.

"I want to hear you pray, Turk. I'll give you that much time. A prayer before you die!"

I was surprised to find that there was no fear. I knew I was going to die and there was nothing I could do about it. I stared, as though hypnotized, as the gun muzzle came down on a line with my eyes, and behind it Slack's face bobbed up and down as he nodded with that same grin, deformed by his scars.

I had heard that when old people are about to meet death, they expect it and have developed an attitude of calm waiting. The same feeling seemed to have taken over my mind. There was no fear. Only a sense of numbed expectancy.

"Go ahead, Turk," he grated mockingly. "Let's hear what kind of a prayer you can wangle out."

"It'll be to meet you in hell!" I said thickly.

Suddenly the roar of a gun filled the glade, drowning out the girl's wracking sobs and the chuckle of glee that had started to rise in Slack's throat.

Seventeen

Slack's hand twitched and the gun went off. The bullet drove into the dirt between my knees, throwing up a small black geyser. He took a step toward me, knees bent as though carrying a heavy load. The weapon fell from his fingers and his hands went up to the gaping hole in his chest, then fell away bloody. His eyes dropped as though to inspect his fingers, surprise in his face.

Then he pitched sideways and plunged into the dark water. Small waves splashed against the shore for a moment, then receded to a series of ripples with air bubbles rising in the center.

There on my knees I watched, slow horror creeping up from the depths of the black water to envelop me like a cloak. The fear that had been absent moments before suddenly flooded in, driving the breath from my lungs in a strangled gasp, seeking to drown me.

Drake Martin came out of the trees and stood looking at the final bubbles, a derringer clutched in his hand. His face was a flat mask of hatred as he turned to the girl, who was looking toward Slack's resting place, her face pallid. Without seeming to look at her, Martin plunged the miniature pistol into his rear pocket and stooped to sweep up the ripped length of printed cotton and wrap it about her.

"Christ, am I glad you showed up!" I finally managed to say. I got slowly to my feet, but my knees were shaking so badly that I was barely able to make it to a tree, where I stood leaning, drawing air into my lungs.

Drake ignored me, staring into the girl's face.

"Where're your clothes?" he asked harshly. Dumbly she motioned to a fallen tree half-hidden by brush. He turned and walked to the thick trunk, grabbing up the riding costume, bringing it back to Malia, who had followed him with her eyes. The bubbles were no longer rising from the depths, and even the ripples had quieted. It seemed like a bad dream, except for the fact that somewhere down in the darkness, I knew, Jeff Slack's lifeless body was floating.

Slowly I moved away from the tree and stooped to pick up Slack's gun. I stared at it for a moment, seeing the smoothly oiled parts and the filed-down hair trigger. Then I turned to hurl it into the pool. Malia started, trembling, her eyes going to the splash, and Martin turned to look at me with a blank, distant expression.

"Get your clothes on," he told the girl quietly, looking back at her. She took the blouse and riding skirt listlessly and turned toward the heavy brush, but was interrupted by the sound of crackling twigs and the snort of a horse.

Martin whirled, too, his hand going to his pocket where the derringer rested, but brought it back to his side as Hollman and Kimo rode out of the approaching darkness to pull up their mounts. The rancher sat stiffly in his saddle, eyes sweeping the scene for a moment before they rested on Malia.

"You heard what he said, Malia. Get your clothes on."

His tone was flat and devoid of inflection, but the girl shuddered involuntarily, then turned to disappear behind the fallen tree. Mark Hollman's eyes never left Martin as he slowly dismounted and came forward to halt between us, looking from one to the other.

"Tell it!" Hollman ordered flatly, his eyes settling on me. His face was grim, his lips a tight line slashing across his features. His eyes were smoky with anger and resentment.

"What was the shot? What're you doing here? Both of you!"

"Jeff Slack," I told him, spent fear still making my tongue feel thick and unmanageable. "He was trying for Malia, when I heard her scream. I rode in and took him, but he pulled a gun on me. If it hadn't been for him"—I indicated the younger man with a nod of my head—"I'd be in the bottom of that pool instead of Slack."

He whirled on Martin, eyes narrowing. "You had a gun on you? After knowing my rules?"

Martin nodded, staring at him coldly. At the same instant he reached to his hip pocket and drew the derringer slowly, holding it in the palm of his hand.

"I ought to kill you!" Hollman growled at him, his voice strong with emotion. "Bringing my daughter here and getting her into this mess!"

"You lay one hand on me, Hollman, and I'll use the other barrel on you!" The youth's voice matched the other man's. "That ain't just idle talk!"

Hollman stiffened and the hand with the derringer came up, the finger tightening about the trigger.

"Drake!"

At the sound of my shout, he started, looking away from Hollman. It was all the rancher needed. A fist lashed out and down across the younger man's wrist, and the knuckles of his other hand connected with the point of Drake Martin's chin. He went over backwards, his boot heels catching in the dirt, tripping him as he tried to step back under the blow.

He lay there for a moment, glaring up at us as Hollman scooped up the derringer and threw it into the pond, setting up a new circle of ripples.

"Get up," Hollman ordered, standing over the man as he slowly crawled to his feet. "You're through. Through in the Islands. Get your gear from the camp and report to the ranch in the morning for your pay. I want you out of here on the next boat."

"And if I ain't?" Martin asked the question slowly, as he

rubbed his jaw. A broad bruise was already turning the flesh dark.

"There's a corpse in the bottom of that pool, and there's some law down in Hilo that don't hold with killings any more than where you come from. That explain it?"

Martin stared at him, the cold, unreadable expression coming back into his eyes, then nodded slowly.

"That explains it." His voice was as expressionless as his face.

"Look here, Mark. Don't you realize what he done? He kept Slack from shooting my face off. And you know what'd've happened to your daughter if he hadn't shown up!" I pushed past Martin as I spoke, but Hollman stared at me with hard eyes.

"If he hadn't been meeting Malia here, this'd never of happened. And he was packing a gun even when he knew what my orders were. That settles it."

Hollman turned his back and stood staring toward the brush where his daughter was dressing. Looking at neither of us, Drake Martin bent to pick up his hat, which had been knocked off when Mark had struck him. He pushed it down on his head and walked toward the edge of the trees. I hurried after him and grabbed his arm, turning him about.

"Look, kid. He'll cool off, and I owe you something," I told him. "I'll get it straightened out."

Martin's eyes flickered for an instant, reflecting the same hatred I had seen in them the moment after he stood watching the bubbles in the pool.

"What I done wasn't for you," he muttered huskily and turned to disappear into the trees. A moment later, I heard the crackle of brush as he rode away.

Kimo glanced at me as I came back to the pool, and his eyes were wide with wonder. As he looked back to where Hollman stood facing his daughter, I turned my eyes in that direction. The rancher was speaking softly, his voice filled with emotion.

"I warned you about seeing him. What have you been doing with him in the brush?"

The girl stared at him for a long time, seeming not to hear the words. Suddenly her face crumpled and her hand flashed up to crack across his cheek. He drew back in surprise, but she didn't give him a chance to speak. She slapped him again with the other hand, then whirled to crash into the brush behind her.

"Kimo! Go after her!" Hollman shouted. "Take her home!"

The boy wheeled his horse and rode after the girl, and a moment later I heard the pound of hooves and the slapping of branches. Hollman stood looking after the sounds, head back, listening, before his shoulders slowly sagged into a tired slump.

"Why did she do it?" he said to himself. "Why did she do it?" Then he turned slowly to look in my direction.

"You're through, too, Turk. I thought I could handle you, but I can't." Suddenly he was a tired old man whose hopes had been swept away in a few short moments of violence.

"Why'd you bring me out here?" I asked him slowly. He shook his head, looking away wearily.

"I don't know, Turk. I thought it was to help you. At least, I tried to tell myself that was the reason. Way down inside, though, I suppose it was to try to prove to myself that I was right in leaving and you were wrong."

"Did you prove anything?" I couldn't keep the smile off my lips at the question, and I knew it was cruel in spite of the fact that I didn't want it to be.

"No." He paused, staring a long way off. Twenty years into the past. "Not the things I wanted to prove, at least."

He started toward his horse, stumbling as though drunk. He didn't look back as he mounted and started to ride into the thick undergrowth, shoulders sagging.

The smile was still on my lips, but I felt sorry for him.

Eighteen

The bunkhouse was deserted when I rode in, and most of the horses were gone from the corral. For a moment I thought that Hollman might have turned out the whole crew to look for Malia, since I saw neither her mount nor Kimo's. Then I remembered that it was payday and the entire crew was in town, including Joe Tam.

They would come riding in about dawn, nursing hangovers and swearing never to ride down to Hilo again. But as soon as the cook threw together a meal, they would be back in the saddle, ready for the day's work, waiting for orders.

Only tomorrow, I realized grimly, someone else—probably Hollman himself—would be laying out the chores for them. I'd be in Hilo, checking a boat schedule.

I had ridden back slowly, allowing Mark to get a good start on me. In his mood, it was better for him to ride alone. Now, as I turned my own horse into the corral, I saw his horse standing in a corner, head pointed at the ground, sides coated with the foam of sweat. Another two miles, and the animal would have dropped under him.

The house was dark, too, except for a single light burning in the office, and I wondered whether Himmler was there with him or if he was licking his emotional wounds by himself.

I went into the bunkhouse and touched a match to the wick of the coal-oil lamp, looking about. A feeling of nostalgia swept over me as I realized this night would be the last time I would see it. And, with the *paniolos* pouring whiskey dents into their month's pay, I wouldn't be going to sleep to the sound of friendly banter over the nightly fantan game.

I was going to miss a lot of things. The feeling of doing a useful job with responsibility; I hadn't realized until then that I liked the feeling. Of seeing Kimo's grin whenever he finished a chore he had been assigned and I told him it was well done. I was going to miss this room with the raw log walls, the pitted dirt floor and its rickety bunks. It was the nearest thing to a home I had had in a lot of years.

I cursed myself for the moment of softness and pushed the thoughts out of my mind. My battered rawhide suitcase was beneath my bunk and I pulled it out, jerking the straps free and spreading it open on the blanket.

I started to take the clothing from the nails in the wall above the bunk, folding each item slowly and putting it into the suitcase. My earlier feeling was engulfed in a heavy shadow of bitterness as I looked at the contents. All these years, and this was what I had to show. This and a second-hand saddle hanging on a corral rail outside!

As I pushed down one of the shirts my hand found the hard bulk underneath, and slowly I reached beneath the cloth to pull it free. The leather holster was still heavy with oil in spite of the years, and the six gun fit snugly in its grasp, yet, when I grasped the notched butt and pulled it free, it slipped smoothly out of the leather.

This was what had brought it all about. A piece of metal and ivory with no life of its own, but the power of life and death for others. This, and a man named Samuel Colt, had cost me a lot. Between them, they had cost me nearly half of my life. They and the kid with the quick hand who had walked down the middle of a dirt street to prove in the bright morning sun that he was right and another man with another gun was wrong. The boy, who was me, seemed like a bad dream now, along with the sudden realization that both of us had been wrong. I had known, as the sheriff clamped handcuffs on my wrists, telling me of the other man who had died in the hail of flying lead, that neither of us had proved a thing.

There was a sound outside and my hand gripped the age-yellowed ivory butt unconsciously. Then I heard the sound of uncertain steps and turned to push the six gun back into the holster, drop it into the suitcase and shut it. I was belting the straps on the bag, when Mark Hollman spoke behind me.

"Reckon I was a little quick up there, Sam," he said slowly. "You'd better unpack and plan on sticking around."

I didn't say anything, didn't turn, but pretended to still be busy with the suitcase as he came further into the room.

"Guess I kind of blew up, didn't I?" he said, apology in his voice. "You've still got the job. You're still foreman." He waited for me to answer, then went on, when I didn't. "You *are* going to stay, ain't you?"

"Nope." I turned then to look at him. He was standing beside the table, staring at the lantern with the resentful attitude of a moth that has just singed its wings.

"Why not?" he asked without looking at me. He had a large gourd in his hand and he was drunk.

"I don't know exactly," I told him slowly, searching my own mind for reasons. They weren't hard to find. "I always figured a man had to have respect for whoever was his boss. You don't fit in that category anymore."

He sat down heavily on one of the benches at the table and ran a finger around the carved fantan number, his eyes still on the lamp.

"She didn't come back, Turk."

"Yeah. I know. Kimo isn't back either. You want to pay me now or in the morning?"

"Whichever you want," he said slowly. "You in that big a hurry?"

"I'll be riding out early, so it might as well be now. I'll leave the horse at the hotel, and you can have Kimo or somebody bring it back."

"Have a drink with me, Sam." It was almost a plea.

I walked over and sat down opposite him at the table. He shoved the gourd toward me, still staring into the flickering light. His eyes were red and unseeing in the light, and I wondered whether he had been crying. I drank from the container, feeling the hot liquor burn at my throat as I pushed it back to him. He tilted it back and gulped down several swallows.

"I didn't mean some of the things I said up there," he ventured tentatively. It was as though he was feeling for an answer, asking approval for the confession.

"If she's your daughter, you shouldn't even have thought them."

He looked at me then, shaking his head slowly. "Sometimes, I don't know what I think, Sam. This is one of those times. I wish she'd come home so I could tell her that."

"You're like a blind man on a merry-go-round, Mark. You're trying for a brass ring, but you don't know where it is. Don't even know for certain what it looks like. The harder you try, the less you know."

"Do *you* know?"

I shook my head. "No. No I don't, but I hope you find it, whatever it is." I stood up and looked down at him. His eyes had gone back to the lantern.

"If you'd like to send Himmler down here with my money, I'd appreciate it. I need some sleep before I pull out."

He rose, nearly falling over the bench, then held out his hand. "I may never see you again, Sam," he said softly. "I'm sorry. I don't know exactly why, but I am."

I shook his hand and watched as he staggered toward the door. A few minutes later, Himmler came with my money and counted the bills out on the table before me.

"Thanks," I said as I scooped up the money and stuffed

it into my shirt pocket. He stood there and I looked up at him. He was frowning at me.

"Something else?" I asked, my voice sarcastic.

"I don't know what this is all about, Turk. Maybe I don't want to know." He shook his head. "But I want you to know that I don't hold anything against you." He seemed embarrassed by his own words. "About that fracas between us. I can see why you thought it might have been me. You know. The rifle and all."

"Forget it. Tomorrow, when I ride out, it won't matter to either one of us," I told the strange, thin man. He smiled, his eyes crinkling behind the thick lenses, and thrust out his hand.

"God go with you, Turk." His voice was low and warm. I gripped his hand, and he turned to hurry out into the night. I sat wondering how much he really thought about God, then I got up and went to my bunk, lifting off the bag and laying down, still fully clothed.

I awoke with a start as I felt fingers brushing my shoulder. I reached out to grab a wrist, and there was a gasp of pain as I twisted it.

"Sam! Sam, listen to me!" It was Malia's voice coming out of the darkness in a frantic whisper. The lamp was out, and I wondered whether all of the fuel had been burned or she had put it out before waking me.

"What is it?" I growled at her.

"You have to get out of here," she said. "He's coming after you. He said he's going to kill you!"

I swung my feet over the bunk and rose, my hand coming in contact with one of her heaving breasts. She pulled away as I brushed past her.

"You have to listen to me," she said, speaking aloud for the first time. "He's like a madman! He says he came here to kill you and he's going to do it before he leaves!"

"It'll wait till I get a light," I told her. "Where's Kimo? Have you seen him?"

"I just woke him. He's saddling your horse now," she said. "There's no time to lose!"

I found the lamp on the table, the chimney still warm. Kimo must have put it out when he came in. I was surprised that I hadn't heard him. I removed the glass, touched a match to the wick, then replaced it, turning to look at the girl.

Her hair was stringy and unkempt, although the mud had been combed out of it. She was staring at me wide-eyed, breathing heavily, as she reached out to grip my arm.

"You have to go, Sam! He was going to get a gun. Then he said he was coming for you!"

"Who? Martin? Why should he want to kill me? When'd you leave him?"

"Just a little while ago. He rode partway back to the ranch with me. He tried all the way to get me to leave with him tomorrow. When I told him I couldn't, that my father needed me, he went crazy!"

"It's all crazy! You, too," I told her sharply. "Drake's nothing but a lovesick kid. That doesn't turn him into a killer!"

"It's his father." She was close to tears, hysteria closing in to shake her words. "He said you killed his father!"

An old scene flashed through my memory. A dirt street. A dead man lying in the dust. The sheriff and his handcuffs. And another body lying in a doorway, while somewhere a child was screaming in pain. Then the courtroom, with the boy staring at me from the witness stand, telling how his father had been killed by a bullet during the gunfight. And the bandage that was still on his cheek.

That boy was Drake Martin!

The shot at me after I'd been released from prison! And the man asking about me in Santa Fe! Then in San Francisco! That had been Martin, too!

As I turned and headed toward my bunk, Malia tried to block me, clawing at my arm, but I pushed her away.

"Sam! You can't!" she screamed. "Take the horse and get away, but don't kill him!"

I jerked the suitcase from the other bunk, tearing at the leather straps. As the bag fell open, I grabbed for the gun-belt and whipped it about my waist.

The girl launched herself at me, clawing at my middle, trying to rip away the weapon, screaming through her sobs.

"Don't, Sam! Don't kill him! I'll go away with you. You wanted me once. I'll go away with you and we'll never see this place again!"

I pushed her away, and she stood looking at me, shocked behind her tears that I didn't accept the bargain.

"It wouldn't work, Malia." My tone was harsh, brittle in my ears. "You're in love with him. If we left, I'd be looking over my shoulder for the rest of my life, expecting him to show up. You'd be looking, and hoping he would!"

"You can't kill him, Sam." She said it slowly, as though offering a final judgment.

"I can't let him kill me!"

She came at me again, trying for my eyes with hooked fingers, her teeth fastening in my neck, as she screamed. There was nothing else I could do as I tore her away. I hit her, and she went catapulting into my bunk.

I looked down at her, wanting to touch her, to tell her I was sorry. She was sobbing hysterically as I turned and headed for the door. Outside, dawn was just breaking.

Nineteen

The sounds from the bunkhouse faded as I walked toward the corral, then halted, ears attuned to the sounds on the night air. A horse was approaching at a run.

Looking toward the enclosure, I could see Kimo leading a horse through the lowered bars, but he halted and looked up at the sound of the approaching animal. Drake Martin loomed up out of the gray of the approaching day as I stepped behind the giant fern and waited. He pulled his winded mount to a halt and leaped to the ground, a dark shadow running the few steps to where the boy stood.

"Where's Turk?" he asked harshly, grabbing Kimo's shoulder and shaking him roughly. "What're you doing with that horse?"

"I look for Malia," the boy lied fearfully. "She no come back. Mister Hollman send me to look."

"Don't lie to me! Where is he?" With his free hand, he slapped the Hawaiian back and forth across the face, his hatred-scarred voice hurling curses.

"No see him," the boy cried. "Just go look for Malia."

Martin was slapping the boy again, as I stepped up behind him and smashed the gun barrel across the back of his head in a quick, slashing motion. He grunted heavily as he released his hold on the lad's shoulder and crashed face down to the ground. The boy fell back against a corral upright, breathing heavily, trying to fight back the tears. In spite of Martin's attack, he hadn't released his hold on the reins. Now I grabbed them from him.

"Thanks, Kimo. Thanks for the lie."

He nodded quickly, gulping back tears. "Malia tell me to saddle your horse, tell no one. I no tell."

I reached out to squeeze his shoulder, and he straightened, trying to force a grin.

"I know, boy. You did me a favor, too. You maybe kept me from having to kill him." I glanced to where Martin lay, his hat crumpled beneath my blow. "You can do one last thing for me, if you will."

"Sure, Mister Turk." He nodded eagerly. "I help you. You speak."

"Just one thing. When this stupid bastard wakes up, you tell him I'm going to kill him!"

The boy stiffened, looking worriedly toward the still form. "Maybe him already dead," he opined. "Maybeso you not have to shoot him by'mby." He had lapsed into the guttural pidgin English.

"I didn't hit him that hard. But you be sure to tell him, when he comes around. Understand? If he tries to follow me, he's dead!"

He nodded gravely. "I tell 'im, you betcha!"

I patted him on the shoulder and turned to mount the horse. In a brief instant I recalled how hard the animal had been ridden the day before and wished that the boy had thought to saddle a fresher mount. I turned to glance over my shoulder as I rode away, and he raised his hand in a single forlorn salute. I waved back, then sank the spurs into the horse's belly and leaned over its neck.

I was running again! Twice I had thought I was free. When I had seen Slack board the boat in Hilo, I thought that it was over. Then, when I had seen him plunge into the pool with Drake Martin's bullet in him, I had the same thought.

And all the time it had been Martin. The kid with the scar

on his cheek and the hatred in his heart, hiding his true feelings behind an expressionless face and a closely guarded mouth. Each time he had looked at me, he knew and took strange pleasure in the fact that I was afraid, and he had added to that fear whenever possible.

The slashed cinch strap during the cattle drive, when I was nearly drowned. Had he meant for me to die then? Or had it been just a cat-and-mouse game gone wrong? And the bullet neatly packaged and delivered to me at the Christmas *luau*. That was from him, too. I remembered the surprised look on Jeff Slack's face, when I had accused him of that move in the Golden Dragon.

But something about Martin had changed, and it was Malia who had changed it. Some of the hardness had gone out of him during the times he had been with her. He had laughed and talked, forgetting his reason for coming to the Islands. Forgetting me, perhaps, until Hollman's jealousy of his daughter and the orders to keep Drake away from her had brought a stream of resentment flooding back, and that emotion had been nurtured into hatred, added to the old passion that had lain dormant, giving it new life.

That was something else for which I could thank Mark Hollman, I thought bitterly. But now he probably would never know. Not that it would matter to him. He had problems of his own. Like trying to figure a reason for Mark Hollman! For his right to live, to exist. Nothing else would matter to him, but that answer!

Dimly I realized that the horse had slowed and that its sides were heaving heavily against my legs. Glancing down, I was surprised to find that the animal was white with sweat along his neck and the deep muscles of his forelegs. Breath was coming from his nostrils in a series of snorts. As I pulled the animal to a walk, I glanced back over my shoulder, scanning my back trail. I was surprised that there was no sign of a rider. Then I cursed myself for thinking there would be.

Turning, I realized for the first time that I had sent the horse plunging away from the ranch without course, without thinking. Now, as the morning sun burned hot on my shoulders, I was at the foot of the trail leading up to the bench pasture. I cursed again, knowing that I had passed the pool where Slack's body must now be floating. I should have halted long enough to water the horse, but it was too late to turn back.

I pulled up, allowing the animal to drop its head and nuzzle at the dew-dampened grass, as I glanced back again. I should have ridden for Hilo, catching the first boat out, but instead, I had allowed panic to be my guide.

Slowly I urged the horse up the trail, kicking at his flanks with my unspurred heels. A plan was shaping in my mind. Once over the volcano, I could cut for the other end of the Island, perhaps to Kona, and find a boat there. If the horse held out that long.

The horse was panting again, his head dropping against the pull of the bit as we reached the pasture and I rested him again, my eyes sweeping the bench for signs of the cattle. Another wave of bitterness swept over me as I saw them grouped in the shade of an overhanging cliff several hundred yards away. Somewhere behind, a man was riding to try to kill me, and I worried about Hollman's cows!

There was a rustling sound in the brush nearby and I whirled, hand to pistol, thumb across hammer. I relaxed as the sound was repeated and the small animal scampered away. Then a new thought struck me and I cursed aloud, causing the horse to raise its head in question.

I had been so quick to run that I hadn't even thought to take Martin's gun. After I had hit him and he lay there with his face in the dust, all I had to do was take the six gun from the holster at his hip. Instead, I had bolted! I had ridden a horse nearly to death to escape a threat that could have been smothered simply by lifting a piece of metal from a man's belt!

Still cursing aloud, I pushed the weary horse across the flat, while a myna bird whistled a mocking answer. The horse stumbled as he started up the lava trail toward the top of the volcano, then almost went to his knees, squealing in pain.

I knew what had happened before I swung down from the saddle and lifted his hoof. The steel shoe was gone, and already the foot was ragged from contact with the rough lava. A long sliver protruded from the animal's hock and he jerked with pain, swinging his head to bite at my shoulder as I pulled it free.

I dropped the hoof and picked up the reins, starting to lead the animal, but he stumbled again, limping after me. He was useless. Too lame to ride.

Turning to glance down the face of the height to the flat bench spread below, I saw the dark figure of a horseman just clearing the trees. I couldn't identify him at that distance, but I knew it was Martin.

Panic gnawed at my nerves, and the six gun jerked into my hand. The front sight was centered on the figure below, my finger tight on the trigger before I realized the bullet wouldn't come within a thousand yards of him. The shot would only serve to reveal my position.

Martin halted and was studying the ground, reading my trail in the still wet grass. As he spurred forward, reining toward the path leading upward to me, I realized that someway he had gotten a fresh horse, which explained how he had overtaken me so rapidly.

The gelding was standing with head bowed, nuzzling his sore foot as I turned to grab the reins, looking up and down the trail. There was a bend about seventy-five yards ahead and I led the animal toward it as rapidly as I could, my thoughts piling over each other as I worked out a plan.

As I turned the sharp bend which hid my back trail, I dropped the reins and left the horse standing there, tossing his head nervously. I ran back along the length of trail, looking for a hiding place, spotting one of the lava tubes which ran into the mountain from the rough path.

I dodged into it and squatted in the shadows, taking my six gun from its holster and spinning the cylinder. My hands shook as I recalled how long it was since the weapon had been fired. The five bullets it now carried were nearly twenty years old. They had been in my cartridge belt when I was arrested, and I had used them to load the weapon after that first try on my life.

What if they had gone dead? Wouldn't fire?

Crouched in the cave, which extended for untold depths into the mountain behind me, I slipped the weapon in and out of the holster, renewing the feel of the butt in my hand, the balance of the deadly weight. Recognition seemed to flow into my fingers, renewing an old friendship, and again I recalled the words of the little gray man at Huntsville: *"Guns are like bad women. You may leave them alone, but you never forget what they're like!"*

The sound of steel ringing on rock echoed through the cavern, wiping the thought from my mind, and I stepped back from the opening as a dark shadow was cast across it, then the feet of Martin's horse and his spurred boots were framed for an instant below the low ceiling. As he passed, I edged forward, looking after him.

He was riding cautiously, gun in hand, glancing warily about for sign of a trap. I waited until he neared the blind bend in the trail, then stepped into the open.

As he reached the curve and saw my lame horse beyond, he jerked up in surprise, then dived from the saddle, his eyes darting about. He stiffened as he saw me. The gun swung toward me and dust splintered off a rock three feet away. My own hand leaped to the holster at my waist, and the gun barrel blurred up for the front sight to rest on him as he fired again.

As I pulled the trigger, I realized that something was all wrong. His stance was awkward and unbalanced. This wasn't a gunfighter I was facing. This was a hate-crazed kid with a gun in his hand he hardly knew how to hold!

The six gun bucked in my hand and Martin was driven backwards against the flank of his horse, his own weapon flying away. The animal snorted, leaping away in surprise, and Drake Martin rolled loosely to the trail, his body sending up a small puff of volcanic ash.

Twenty

Drake Martin spun under the impact of my bullet and fell face down in the trail. The lava ash was settling in his blond hair as I walked slowly toward him, my finger holding the slack in the trigger. As I drew close to him, I thumbed back the hammer and saw a shudder run through his body, and the fingers of his outstretched right hand twitched spasmodically.

I kicked the gun away from him, then stepped back.

"You can quit playing possum, boy," I told him bluntly.

"Go ahead. Shoot me, but it'll have to be in the back," he declared bitterly, his mouth muffled in the dust. "I ain't going to roll over for your benefit."

He inhaled sharply, and his body stiffened with pain as the shock from the bullet passed. Then he relaxed and I knew he was unconscious. Still cautious, I stepped around the body and dug a toe into his ribs. He jostled loosely, and I pushed the toe under his shoulder and jerked it up abruptly. I was on the uphill side of the trail. The momentum carried him over on his back.

His face appeared white and drawn behind his tan, and I realized for the first time, seeing them stand out against the pallid background, that he had freckles. He looked a lot like the little boy in that courtroom a long time ago who had told a jury how his father died while watching a gunfight. The scar running along his cheek was red and angry-looking.

The bullet had caught him high in the right shoulder and was buried somewhere inside. Judging from the path it had taken, I figured that it had broken his shoulder blade and might be lodged in the bone.

I pushed his hat beneath his head as a pillow, then reached up to tear his shirt from around the wound, ripping out a section of the front panel to swab away the matted blood. I left the cloth pressed against the free-flowing wound as I stood up, glancing about for water.

A hollow in one of the lava outcroppings held some of the rain water, and I used a strip from my own shirttail to sponge it up, turning back to the boy.

His eyes were open, puzzled and wary, as he watched me walk back to where he lay. A glint caught my eye and I stared out over the trail to the flat below. Two horses, their riders bent low over their necks, were galloping across the open strip toward the foot of the mountain. I knelt and rubbed the wet rag gently across the puckered bullet hole.

"How do you feel?" I asked.

"Like I've been shot. How *should* I feel?" His voice was sullen, but there was a note of wonder hidden in it. The note grew stronger as he asked, "Why're you doing this, Turk?"

I shook my head, keeping my eyes on the wound. "I don't know." And I really didn't.

"You know I'll still get you when I get the chance, don't you?" he said, some of the venom trying to creep back into his voice. "This ain't going to help you none!" He attempted to sit up, but I pushed him back and he winced against the pain, his face twisting in a grimace.

"You won't get another chance," I told him quietly, "'cause you're going to hear me now and you're going to hear me real good. Your old man got killed by an accident that was more his fault than mine. Any damned fool should know that if he can see a gun, the gun can see him and he can get hurt."

His good hand went up to brush the scar on his cheek, but if he was trying to draw attention to it, it went ignored.

"Whoever was to blame, I spent eighteen years of my life paying for that mistake. I don't figure to pay no more. Eighteen years can be a lot more than a lifetime under some circumstances."

He was staring at me out of slitted eyes as I raised him to a sitting position and pushed him back so he could lean against a rock. I turned to glance down toward the bench below, looking for sign of the riders, but they had disappeared beneath the overhanging ledge.

"You're young, Drake. You have a whole life ahead of you, and in country like this you can carve out your whole future. You've got a girl that loves you enough that she offered to go away with me to keep you from getting shot. Marry someone like that, and you could go a long way."

His lip curled cynically and he snorted. "Marry her, hell. I'd have to marry her old man along with her!"

"You just go ahead and put a ring on her finger and ignore Mark Hollman. He's a tired old man, and before long he'll realize he's worse than that: a tired, lonely old man. He'll come around."

He was staring at me, scowling and licking his lips nervously. "You're forgetting something, Turk. I still figure I owe you something."

"You just now tried it and lost, or don't you feel that bullet so good?" My voice was harsh as I stood up, looking down into his upturned face. "Malia and Kimo are on the way up here now. They'll get you to a doctor and get you patched up, but there's something I want you to think about. I could have killed you this time without half trying."

He started to speak but I cut him off roughly. "I got just

one more thing to say. I'm leaving the Islands, but you're staying. I don't know yet where I'm going, but if I ever see you again I'll kill you on sight! Understand?"

He continued staring up at me for a long moment, then nodded, looking down at his shoulder. I turned to walk to where his horse stood, the grounded reins keeping it there.

"One more thing," I told him, as I turned to look back. "I'm taking your horse. Mine's too beat to make it any further." He was still staring at me through narrowed eyes, his face set in that old, familiar expression, showing no emotion at all. I spurred the horse to the blind turn in the trail and turned to glance back at him once more.

"So long, kid."

"So long, Turk." The voice was so low I could hardly hear it, but I thought I caught a ghost of a smile on his lips before the lava outcropping cut him off from my sight.

As I spurred up the trail, cutting along the side of the mountain, I heard a cry behind me and recognized it as Kimo's voice, knowing he and the girl had found Drake.

As I reached the high point on the jagged trail, where one side fell away to a sheer drop of several hundred feet, I pulled up the horse, and my hand went to the weight at my hip. Slowly I unbuckled the gunbelt, slipped it from about my waist and held it up to look at it.

Far off, bright in the morning sun, I could see the blue-gold of light on water and wondered if somewhere out there I might not find another island. An island where a man might live in peace and never have to worry, never have cause to look back over his shoulder, wondering what nameless fear was behind him, seeking to catch up.

I looked at the gunbelt again, my eyes holding on the notches carved in the ivory butt for a long moment before I allowed it to slip from my hand. I sat listening as it bounced down the face of the cliff, the sound echoing back to me from the depths until it faded.

"*Guns are like bad women,*" the man had said, but somewhere there might be a good woman. And there just might be that island. My eyes were on the distant sea, as I dug a heel into the horse's flank, forcing him to a trot.